About the author

Taonaya Fleury grew up with the constant fascination of life and the origin of it. Many nights she sat on the roof of her childhood home, staring out into the universe, wondering if there was more to know, to discover.

This inquisitiveness led her on a journey to research the many religions of the world, as well as history, science, philosophy, and even outlying secular theories.

Her passion for the unknown resulted in this book. A fiction based on a string of ideas that may carry with it... a seed.

SEED

Taonaya Fleury

SEED

Vanguard Press

A CIP catalogue record for this title is
available from the British Library.

ISBN 978 1 78465 980 6

*Vanguard Press is an imprint of
Pegasus Elliot MacKenzie Publishers Ltd.*
www.pegasuspublishers.com

First Published in 2022

**Vanguard Press
Sheraton House Castle Park
Cambridge England**

Printed & Bound in Great Britain

Dedication

I dedicate this book to our Source, which we all derive from.

To my father, Claude, for he taught me of all the wonders of life and beyond. For instilling in me the beauty of imagination and wonderment.

To my mother, for her unconditional love.

To my family, for their continuing love, support and sharing in the wonderment of our existence.

To the many people I've encountered in my life who knowingly, and unknowingly, bestowed upon me the magic of connectivity.

Acknowledgements

Special thank you to Debbie Ann Hill for reviewing my final draft.

Chapter 1
In Search of

I was waiting, just like every other scout, in the West Botanic Garden about a mile away from the main Council Hall. It had been hours since I came here, and I had spent another hour staring at the Hemploid plant which was the main focus of our study in the West Botanic Garden. The little herb that grew no taller than a foot had properties unlike the other thousands of floral species that covered a great part of The Trinity.

I looked up at the artificial ceiling and wished for a moment to see the sky instead.

The Trinity is my home. It is the home to the most advanced race in half of the universe. *I think.* I reside on one of the planets which form The Trinity. The Cygnus Solar System houses more than twenty different planets besides The Trinity but unfortunately, the other planets don't house species more interesting than a few evolved forms of the four-legged mammals we sometimes import for research.

I gather a small amount of pollen from one of the newest flowers that has opened on a Hemploid plant near me. I press my finger on the edge of my belt and make a small cut on it while making my way to sit by the edge of one of the small ponds. I rub a tiny amount of pollen onto the fresh wound on my finger. In a matter of seconds, the tiny cells that were apart momentarily, had completely healed, in fact my hand never felt better. I smile to myself. This little plant had always amazed me, even as a child when my father would bring me to one of the laboratories on base to educate me.

I look behind me and see the other scouts talking with each other, discussing the predicaments that the Council had put them in. We all knew what would be disclosed in the Hall once the meeting was over, but there is no rule forbidding thinking against the obvious outcome, *yet.* I walk ahead of the group of scouts that had gathered near me, I wanted some peace of mind, so I walk out of the east exit towards the wide-open area which marked the boundary of this institution. One of the biggest structures in the entire continent, the Council Hall was only a part of this massive joint which was consolidated and dedicated to different departments. The East Wing comprised a huge structure solely dedicated to Technological Advancement and Relief. The North Wing comprised the Scouting Academy along with a section that contained an overwhelming number of scouting ships.

These scouting ships were the best that the researchers here could come up with; provided with a self-sustainable power source, the scouting ships could undertake expeditions running up to twenty years or more. State-of-the art accommodations, ultra-modern medical services and a short list of distasteful food. Space food sucks. There were several reasons why I didn't want to go on another expedition, let alone a longer one. I had just completed my twentieth round, but it makes me wonder. Every scout that has been commissioned here has experience of over fifteen expeditions. This means that this mission has a chance of being enthralling, like the other last five missions I have been commissioned to.

I bend over the stone fence and witness the glory of what we have accomplished and what we have yet to accomplish, if there was anything left to do. As long as I can remember, I have only seen this world moving forward and faster after every breakthrough. It gets tiring sometimes, seeing the same faces for hundreds of years, growing at a snail's pace, maybe even slower. This was the primary reason I wanted to join the Academy just like my father did. This was the only way I could escape the familiarity of this planet and fill my long life with new discoveries and knowledge.

How much more could we evolve? I wondered. We had lived so long, our kind, me, that the thought of what would be next was unfathomable. Yet, we knew that throughout our many phases of existence, it had occurred several times over already. That is, how we even came to The Trinity. We were not always here. Stories were told of our arrival from another time in space, but for reasons only known to the Elders, the full story of our arrival was never revealed. We just had to learn to exist in what was now and not what had been, nor what was to be. Otherwise, our souls would never have been able to be at peace, and in this type of consciousness.

Whenever I think about the beginning, my thoughts would turn towards the life I have right now. The life of a scout is nothing more than an extended version of a researcher, overlooking and observing what happens to petri dishes in a laboratory. But instead of observing something really closely that is just a few inches away from us, the scouts observe and report viable information from distant planets and galaxies millions of light years away from The Trinity. The Elders, which are the oldest and wisest celestial beings, were the first beings to inhabit the planet. They were the ones who later formed The Trinity. They sent hundreds of ships out into the vast space to discover and learn about the inhabitants of these widely scattered planets. For millennia, the Elders have sent branches of our species and civilization in the form of observers and messengers to millions of planets across the universe.

Planting the seed of our existence, along with extracting information and using it to establish an advanced society, has been the purpose of the Elders. For aeons, the celestial beings have dedicated their superior intelligence and methods into becoming the most advanced race in the ever-expanding cosmos.

We exchanged social values as well as many

resources that resided on the three planets which the celestial beings had inhabited. Each one with a unique topography of its own; the beings adapted to the environment of all three and thus made The Trinity, which connected the core of the three planets through energy receptors placed deep in the crust of each planet. One of the many gifts that the Elders had was the gift of having an exceptionally long life. Even though we are gifted with life which seems like it would never end, it does deplete. The process just goes by so slowly that it remains unnoticed.

After what felt like millennia of exchange of intellectual knowledge and necessary resources, the Elders formed a society where they could finally practice the expansion of the superior beings they were. Now the planets have thousands of floral Animalia species living in complete sync with the environment that has been artificially transformed to provide every single specie a sustainable atmosphere.

Thinking about the beginning reminds me of how little regard we give to our lives, which are incredibly long, though it is easier to feel disconnected with life if it's led without a purpose. Maybe that's why the Elders structured a system where every being on the three planets, have specific jobs appointed to them that they do during their lifespan. Maybe becoming a scout, a mere tool for discoveries for the Elders, wasn't my choice at all. It might have been incorporated into my brain so that I wouldn't have an option besides thinking that the roots originally lay within my own conscience.

I have nothing against the system, but it feels so structured that I haven't been able to exercise free will to any real extent. Like at this very moment, I want to be with someone, somewhere else and yet here I am, waiting to be sent millions of light years away, *again*.

"Tuloriah!" Someone calls behind me, "it's time!" I turn around and see Lharkin waiting for me at the East exit. *"Here we go,"* I say to myself quietly and motion him to move along.

The scouts line up to march towards the Council Hall. The architecture is magnificent, almost incomparable to the ones on the other two planets. However, the highest Council was present on this one and every important decision was made here, among the Infinite Seven.

The Infinite Seven is the group of seven Elders who are said to be the *firsts*. There was nothing before them and they laid the foundation of everything we see here now. I look behind me and Lharkin is giving me an apologetic look. He knows how much I didn't want to go on this expedition, but no one can deny a *direct* order from the Elders.

I feel the blood rushing to my head as we all march into the Great Hall where my destiny awaits me. We stand with respect in the presence of the Infinite Seven. No one has seen them except the people who need to and it is considered a privilege to be in their presence. Even though I've been in their presence more than a dozen times, it still gives me goosebumps. Not once have I seen the light surrounding them fading; it is always warm and pure. Though their physical form has weakened, their astral energy is as strong as I can first remember it.

The scout leader moves to the front and bows down, paying his respect to the Elders. When they nod, he gets up and the meeting starts with The One addressing and paying tributes to each one of us who has given a considerable amount of our lives to their cause of exploration and expansion. The One is the leader by popularity because there is no such thing as conflict in power in The Trinity; no one here fights for power because their roles are already assigned. Each planet has a council of seven members, but the most ancient ones remain here. The three councils, with their supreme power and intellectual approach chose The One who would communicate and represent the unanimous decisions of the council to the concerned authorities.

"The Elders appreciate your efforts to be here on such short notice," The One announces from the center most giant crystal pod which floats high above us along with six other pods, three on each side. They form a semi-circle above us and from these pods the Elders communicated their verdicts.

"It is our honor Elders, the scouts serve your purpose before us and surely will after us," The scout leader responds back in a firm tone.

"The scouts have served us for millennia, pursuing our thirst for knowledge and exploring this infinite universe. For long that has been our only purpose…"

"But…" surprisingly, one of the Infinite Seven spoke instead of The One. That rarely happened.

"We now comprehend that we are running out of space to explore. Our purpose of exploring distant worlds doesn't serve as a purpose any more." I hadn't seen this coming, even though everyone had realized this a long time ago but nobody inferred that the Elders would realize it this soon.

"We feel that a life without a purpose is as lost as a lonely asteroid, traveling the quiet space with no destination. Our existence should never be without a purpose."

"We understand that, Elders," our leader declared, "we have dedicated our lives to serve The Trinity, whatever it may be."

Yes, we did. That was part of our oath when we graduated from the academy.

"However, we would like to be enlightened with what the Council has decided for the purpose of future expeditions," the leader added.

There was a long silence as everyone in the Great Hall became anxious, wondering what our mission would be. I wasn't looking forward to it anyway because I knew that starting a mission on a completely new objective (just like I was expecting of this one) required an unnatural amount of time, which seemed daunting.

"Expansion, scout leader, that is our new purpose." Everyone was taken aback by The One's answer. I looked at Lharkin who looked as surprised as me. "Expansion? What does that even mean? Haven't our kind already set up salvation points in almost a million planets?" My query is almost immediately addressed by the scout leader to the Elders.

"Not expansion of ourselves, scout leader. We will plant extensions of ourselves which will give new meaning to our never-ending life."

"You see," another one of the Infinite Seven took the lead, "we have exhausted all our discoveries, we are in fact, just drifting in time and doing nothing more than filling our archive of knowledge. It is time for evolution."

This was something I hadn't anticipated hearing; the scouts were merely a tool for observation and collection of knowledge. How could we lay the foundation of evolution? And of what? We are the most evolved beings in almost half of the universe!

"For decades, The Council has been pondering over the tactics of laying the foundation of our kind on a primitive planet as an extension of our existence. With an infinite life, even as celestial beings, we cannot understand the value of having a limited lifespan. One can consider it as a long-term experimentation program. That is why we want the best and the experts."

I chewed on my lips; I didn't like where this was

heading. I knew what *"long-term"* meant in our field, they could have just said, *"we are sending you on a mission which has a 10% chance that you'll come back from it in less than a 100 years".*

My mind spaced out to the endless outcomes this expedition would have on my personal life which wasn't going great as it is. It wasn't until Lharkin was shaking my shoulder that I realized, I was being addressed by the Council, *directly. This has never happened before.*

"Ms Tuloriah, you would be an exceptionally perfect fit for this particular mission." I was thoroughly confused.

"I beg your pardon, Elders?" I say and as I do, my leader gives me the death stare.

"Your particular expertise in the extensive research of primitive planets and genetic advancements makes you the perfect candidate for the First Officer position of one of the expedition crew."

I had to process the command of the Elders twice before I could accept it. This was a promotion I didn't think I was going to get for another five missions.

I regain my composure and clear my throat. "What primitive planet if I may ask, Elders?"

My question was followed by a deafening silence, some whispers and exchanged glances among the Elders.

"5118208, Ms Tuloriah, your destination is 5118208." The announcement sends a jolt through my entire body. I know why they assigned me as First Officer for this expedition. It was because I already had attended a mission to 5118208, *with my father.*

"There is nothing on 5118208, Elders. The inhabitant chart only compromises of a limited number of Floral and Animalia specie, far less evolved than ours."

I try to reason with them because literally 5118208 was a lost cause when it came to finding any sort of signs of potential evolution or even advancement. 5118208 was a planet at the farthest end of the universe from us, revolving around a yellow star with nothing much to offer to our kind.

"We understand your concerns Ms Tuloriah but the Council wants to look towards a primitive planet which has amicable conditions. Your genetic expertise is a gift, and the Council has decided to rely on your observations regarding survival tendencies of planted biological life."

I couldn't believe it, *5118208* of all places. Included as one of the most distant planets from The Trinity, this was a complete nightmare. I had to agree, I had no other choice.

"Yes Elders, my father and I did two expeditions in that part of space until the unfortunate incident. We gathered much information about its topography and geological conditions," I add.

"The Council would like the scouts to conduct in-depth research this time. Collecting samples from the surface and experimenting on potential survival of a genetically modified specie."

"We understand, Elders. The Council's decisions are indisputable, and we will make preparations right away," the scout leader declared before I could say any more about it.

"Very well," The One concludes and we are asked to leave the scout leader in the Great Hall and go prepare for the long journey.

I sit, dazed in the West Botanic Garden. This expedition seemed like a long and tedious affair and somehow, I don't know why but I was feeling dull even thinking about it. I didn't like the idea of leaving them for such a long time. I had no idea what this expedition would mean to me. I had been promoted to the rank of First Officer and would be the first along with my crew to set foot on 5118208. In the past, we had just observed. Seeing it from a distance. Our reports indicated that it didn't promise much in terms of technological discoveries, we never bothered to expand the research. This was a privilege and a drag at the same time.

"That was unexpected; congratulations, Tuloriah." Lharkin broke my train of thought as he sat beside me.

"This is anything but celebratory, Lharkin," I replied, looking at him remorsefully. He chuckles but then falls silent again.

"This is something beyond us, Tuloriah. I think we have been chosen to be part of something legendary and evolutionary. Study of genetically modified beings for another planet? You don't hear that one every day," he states.

"I know Lharkin, this is a big responsibility but also a sacrifice as well. This is more than an expedition, I'm afraid we are getting into a lifelong commitment with this one," I say.

"Not that we have an issue with life being too short to get the job done!" he adds as we both laugh, nervously. He was right, time is irrelevant here. There is no hurry for anything because one has all the time in the universe. Sometimes, I wonder what it could have felt like to experience things in the frame of a limited life span and intelligence. How would we live? How would we react when we know that our bodies are extremely vulnerable? Would we learn to appreciate the nuances in life if we knew time was limited?

I always wondered whether, in a world as perfect as ours, would there be any possibility to change things even if there isn't a need to? Maybe that's why the Elders have changed the course of their purpose? They want to give life a different meaning which they had lacked because of their exceptionally long life? I've always wondered about these questions and I think I'm on my way to getting close to getting the answers. I feel it in my bones that this is going to change us. I need to play my part well.

"Where do you keep drifting off to?" Lharkin brings my mind back to the present.

"Nothing... I was just wondering what would

traveling back to primitive planets in order to search for a purpose mean for our kind?" I share with him.

He remains silent and then huffs, "I guess we'll just have to see."

I look at him and his calmness amazes me. Maybe because he hasn't been in an *unfortunate* event like I have to develop resistance to being commissioned to somewhere such as *5118208*. My thoughts drift back to what happened, but I immediately shake them off because that story is for another time.

Chapter 2
Discovery

"Tuloriah!" I stumbled to the floor from my seat right at the feet of the officer.

"Ummm Fath— I mean Officer, yes! You needed something?" I stammered, no idea who was standing in front of me. I saw that it was my father, in full uniform, and I immediately lost my composure, almost falling from the chair I slept on.

He looked at me, the corners of his mouth twitching. Me almost calling him '*father*' was not missed by him. He regained his formality and said in a commanding tone, "Tuloriah, I know we are toggling at the edge of the universe with nothing useful to do at the moment but still, we have to keep our eyes open."

My father, the Head Officer of the Research team on Expedition Number 32101-ERS, reminded me of this in a tone which I knew was disguised with false sternness. Fortunately, I was recruited as the Junior Researcher in my father's team, which meant that I got to do the *good stuff* and was let off easy if I got myself into trouble.

"Yes Officer, we've been drifting for so long that it made me feel drowsy," I said sheepishly, trying to present a valid excuse. My father was not a stern man, so he just smiled, nodded and left. I breathed a sigh of relief and sunk into my seat again. I looked out the window across from my little office, situated at the furthest corner of the gargantuan ship. *You are just bored,* I concluded, *you are really bored!*

I looked at the ceiling out of habit. I always do that when I am thinking. I then looked back at the window, seeing the light filtering in by the glow of a distant sun that we were drifting by. It was incredibly beautiful, the space. An infinite canvas where even a small speck of a distant star felt as if it was a work of art, painted on infinite darkness to enhance its beauty.

Right now, we were drifting by the famous yellow sun called '*Sol*'. 'Drifting by' would have been an understatement because we were millions of light years away from it, but still somehow the yellow tinge on the window made me feel warm. I knew that a yellow sun provides warmth if you were at a safe distance. The planet that we were targeting was far enough to be warm, but not so far as to be uninhabitable.

The yellow sun had been a huge part of my father's research because of its beguiling properties. It was the only sun — among the twelve galaxies that made up Sector 12 — that had the least harmful radiation effects. Even though the yellow sun had some of the most aggressive solar flares in the entire sector, it still promised some positive outcomes as well. This became the basis of my father's research and so here we are, on my second expedition as a graduated scout from the academy.

My father proposed that studying the effects of the yellow sun on the nearest planets would further help him get a breakthrough in his research. The Council of the Elders issued permission for leading an expedition to Sol System. For as long as I could remember, my father had been ambitiously working on creating the perfect environment for a genetically modified living organism. For this purpose, he wanted to study the effects of a sun that had the least hostile effects on living organisms So, he petitioned to observe and collect samples from the various planets that revolve around the yellow sun, particularly showing his interests in a planet called *5118208.*

It took him a while to get his request through and by that time, I had come back from my first brief expedition to Sector 20. I had done detailed research on genetic modification and terraforming. This is why my teachers recommended to my father that he take me on as a Junior Researcher. *'She is a rising star, just like you!'* they had said and it made my father so proud to commission his daughter as a researcher for a mission for which he had devoted a considerable amount of time of his life, and also of his intellect.

I tore my gaze from the window and looked at the hologram of JU-216, one of the planets in the Sol System. We had experienced overheating of one of our main engines when we tried to escape the gravity of an asteroid as big as an entire planet, passing us by in close proximity. It is hard to comprehend the situation of a location where the ship will space warp to. So as soon as we warped, we got caught in the gravity of the asteroid. Thankfully, we were able to boost our way out just in the nick of time.

Now, we are using the gravity shift of JU-216 to smoothly slingshot directly to 5118208. In the meantime, the engine cooled off. My father had proposed the name '5118208' when he went on the first expedition to this planet. Although it was brief, it must have been an amazing experience because since then, he has been infatuated with it. There is a *beep,* and the coms go online.

'All units stand by, first descend in T-minus thirty minutes. Pod 829 standing by for deployment.' That was my cue and so I hurriedly made my way towards the hangar where the pod was lined up and ready. I changed into my uniform and quietly went through the sanitation process before taking my place in the pod with four other fellow members. As always, I got the inexplicable feeling of excitement, mixed with apprehension, at what was about to happen. I checked the coms and the hydraulic system before giving the green signal for release. We used pods for surveying and for sample collection as our ships were too big to come so close to the threshold point. The pod fell out of the hangar and into space, where our pilot took manual control.

The pilot eased the pod into the outer portion of the

mesosphere because we were not doing surface sample collection. The research only needed the atmospheric dilution ratio and elemental percentage. I started the particulate suction pump, which was about a foot in diameter. I launched the pump and it immediately started to suck in particulates from the atmosphere. The system had started calculating results and just as the elemental proximity result came through, the coms started to go berserk.

"Mayday! Mayday! Do not return to the ship, repeat do not return to the ship!" Even before responding to the stress call, my hands were frozen to the console as I could see everything in front of me.

They say that traumatic things happen in slow motion, and that was my experience too because everything felt slow. Even my heartbeat had decelerated in that exact moment when the ship's shield decimated a few of the small asteroids that hit it. However, it was in that exact moment I realized what was going to happen. The yellow tinge that I was admiring a few hours ago through the glass window now covered my sight completely. It was not warm; it would have been cold outside in space because only that tinge remained in my mind as everything else was engulfed in a shower of asteroids right before my eyes.

"Tuloriah! Tuloriah!" A voice booms in my ears at the same time as two pair of hands are shaking me. I open my eyes, and that same yellow tinge was still present. I push away the source, whatever it is pouring yellow light into my eyes.

"Get that away from me! You know I don't like that color." I try to sit up, but I feel like my body is completely numb.

"What are you doing out here on the bench?" Lharkin ask as he immediately turns off the torch. I blink my eyes a few times at his question as I could not remember anything except an explosion.

"It looks like you fell asleep here," he replies on my behalf, and I realize that I had indeed fallen asleep on a bench outside of the campus garden. I press my neck and nod in agreement.

"What happened?" I ask.

He eyes me for a few moments and then replies, "I just came up to check on you; we are all set for the expedition. Only you were missing." He looks at me with concern and adds, "You okay?"

I didn't want to think about my dream. I was concerned about it, so I concentrated instead on the millions of stars that were hung up like little diamonds in the sky.

"Bad dream." I reply shortly, and he sighs.

"Tuloriah, this is an opportunity which comes once in a millennium. Laying the foundation of evolution? We should consider ourselves lucky!" Lharkin sounds overly excited, and why would he not be? If my mind were not plagued with such traumatic memories, I would have been as excited as he was.

"I am…" I say and pause for a bit, gathering my

thoughts, "it's just hard to be at that part of the universe knowing what happened last time. But I'm not a pessimist so I'm just going to get prepared for the journey." I get up and leave to make the necessary preparations for the expedition.

The Elders had specifically chosen me because after the tragic accident in Sector 12, I continued my father's work with the information I had gathered at that time. It was true: there was no one on Trinity who had as much research piled up about 5118208 as my father and I did. Promoting me this early meant that the mission had undeniable importance, and I had to carry it out with as much clarity as I could.

We all line up once again in the Great Hall with our supervisors to bid farewell to the Elders. They praise our efforts, commitment and dedication for the mission, which was a proud moment on its own. Being the First Officer meant that most of the research and the surveying team would directly report to me. Although, I would prefer doing the ground work on my own. This expedition was different because for the first time, we would be making contact with the surface. 5118208 was a hostile planet because of the countless Animalia species present, many of which were categorized as carnivorous. We had to be extra cautious about our landing site. However, with our sophisticated technology, it had been predetermined where we would be landing so the expedition was 100% safe.

It was extraordinary that the mission was provided

with the most advanced ship of the three planets. The technological advancement on Venture-88 was unfathomable. Every scout had the widest smile on their faces because this was a dream come true. No one with an experience less than at least fifty expeditions had ever ridden such a stunning piece of technology, but we were among the chosen few who were about to board it. I board the ship along with Lharkin, but we are quickly separated as he is working with the communications team and I am headed towards the research department.

The next few hours are just a blur of endless inspections, double-checking and triple-checking the engines, recalculating designation coordinates, and a million other procedures to make sure that no unfortunate incident happens because of any technical malfunction. Even after thousands upon thousands of expeditions, there is always a probability of 0.0000001% of something going wrong on the mission due to technical malfunctions. We took pride in our accuracy and precision, that is why we were the most advanced race in more than half the universe.

Finally, we get the green signal for take-off and the coms go online.

"Stand by all personnel, launch in T-thirty seconds, requested to follow immediate safety protocol."

So that was it, I take my seat and gesture for the seatbelt to go on. In about thirty seconds, I will be on the most important journey of my life. I could feel it in my bones that this would change my life forever and so, my anxiety turns into shudders when the ship gains enough momentum for a launch. *"This is going to be a long trip,"* I say to myself. Just then, I felt a jolt which pushes me back against my seat, an indication that the ship has entered space warp.

5118208 was as far away from The Trinity as to be at the other end of the universe. Where a normal ship without the space-warp technology would take about a thousand years to reach 5118208, it was going to take us about twenty years to reach it, even with the advanced warping technology the ship was equipped with.

Twenty years! I think to myself *even with the space-warp technology!* It would not be healthy for the crew to warp that far. It would tear our bodies apart. So instead of warping all the way, we would warp to a safe point and travel on boosters until the warp core cools down. In this way, we will not exhaust our resources before preparing for the journey back.

Most of the crew goes into the hibernation pods during abnormally long journeys such as this. I never liked missing out on the astounding view, so I usually go into the hibernation pod halfway through. However, this time I decided to spend my journey peacefully sleeping, so I tell my AI companion to ready my pod. I change my uniform and make my way towards the hibernation pod. I climb the spacious stretcher-like bed and gesture to the AI to commence the initiation process. It only takes me a minute to sweep into a deep and relaxing slumber.

"Father! FATHER!" I shouted from my pod, but my voice could not reach him to tell him that an asteroid was coming their way. The asteroid was too big to be deflected by the shield and hence, it engulfed the whole ship within seconds. Everyone gone, within seconds. We could not do anything at that point. I felt my soul leave my body, numb from the realization that my father was gone. And we were now stuck here with limited power in our pod. Fortunately, the pod had a transmission link to the commanding sector back home. The technology at that time was only enough to send a ship to us in no less than thirty years. Luckily, the engineer that boarded the pod with me was a prodigy. He cross wired the electrical systems to create a short but strong space warp that would save us around twenty years' worth of traveling. However, the intense and long warping caused our bodies to undergo space strain and we *just* survived long enough to be rescued. I still remember the time when I woke up back on Trinity and struggled to breathe, just like I was doing right now.

I open my eyes immediately as the glass hatch was disassembling.

"All personnel stand by, arriving at 5118208 in T-five minutes."

Wow, that was quick. It felt as if I had just gone to sleep. After waking up, I go through the intense medical inspection, as always, for cryo-poisoning, which was a common side effect of long usage of hibernation pods.

I get dressed and go to the captain's bridge for the search team deployment. This time we are taking a smaller ship to 5118208 instead of a pod.

"Ms Tuloriah," the captain greets me as I arrive on the bridge, "I hope your hibernation period went well?"

"Captain," I nod curtly. "Is the ship ready?" I add while checking the coordinates of our landing on the hologram projection screen.

"Yes, if you would, please get your team down to the hangar and we will be all set for deployment." I acknowledge his orders and go straight to the hangar along with my crew of seven people. The team and I gear up, take command of the deploying ship and give the command center the signal. The team rounds up the statuses for the final inspection, and the command center finally deploys the ship.

The ship floats for a second, until the boosters go online, and it races towards 5118208.

"Please advise, Survey Ship SS-20089, flight status?"

"Please be advised Command Center, the ship is locked on coordinates, entering the gravity of the planet, shifting to supersonic," the pilot informs the Command Center through the coms

The ship accelerates towards the surface as the boosters are shifted to supersonic to break into the planet's atmosphere. The ship continues to accelerate until it slows down, which is when the pilot informs us that the ship is near the coordinated location. As soon as the after-effects of the supersonic traveling subside, my breath leaves my lungs as I feast my eyes upon the view outside the window. I have never seen anything like it before: green mountains! There were no green mountains back home.

5118208 seems to be an incredible spectacle of natural beauty. The ground is lush green with spectacular overgrowth; I wonder what kind of floral species I could find here. The scales show high temperature and pressure, which means they would eventually have to survey the ground in protected suits. My father's study showed that 5118208 had a harsh gravity, so that would save us from using the boosters on the suit for walking.

The coordinates showed that the location of our landing was deep within the mountains, where the temperature was comparatively low, and the soil was smooth enough to initiate experimentation.

It was like a complete fantasy, the way we crossed the great mountains, and a few Animalia species flew by our ship, showing off as if the way they were flying was how it was done! Finally, the pilot eases our landing on a spot between two great green mountains in a dense jungle. The landing causes a few of the trees to break apart and create a space for us.

"Command Center, please be advised. SS-20089 has made safe landing on coordinates 22.59.33," the pilot informs the command center.

"This is Command Center, no hostile situation yet

detected, please initiate the ground team."

As the replies patch through, the pilot signals for us to commence with the preparations. The magnificent SS-20089 was lavishly provided with the latest micro-organic studies laboratory, along with a mobile one, which was to be set up on the grounds. Actions that are carried out here in the lab inside the ship would be mimicked in the laboratory set up outside on the grounds. This way, we can control and monitor the experimentation and be safe from the harsh environment as well.

I and two other members suit up to set the ground laboratory. The total time that we would be spending on 5118208 would be close to two years. In order for the genetically modified organism to survive on 5118208, we would need to experiment on all possible combinations of environmental factors so that we can find the ideal one. This meant that we had to stay on 5118208 for a period in which we could study the changing temperature, weather and atmosphere. We had to study the effects based on the time it took 5118208 to complete a single revolution around the yellow sun. Two years because we leave nothing to chance; the study had to be 100% accurate.

The team and I set up a laboratory outside the ship on a patch of clear ground. After that, it was just a long series of sample collection, testing, inspection, experimentation and logging.

Chapter 3
Council

This fruit tasted incredibly delicious. It tingled my taste buds in a way I had never experienced before. Ever since my team and I arrived on 5118208, I had experienced a series of many 'firsts'. 5118208 was distinctively different from The Trinity in many unspoken ways. There was a certain level of freedom and independence here that simply is not present on Trinity, but then again there is no one here except species who only know how to hunt and eat. It is nearly impossible that there may exist a more sophisticated life form than ours in this universe. However, there must be something; a compelling reason behind The Elders wanting us to embark on such a journey.

One thing I have to admit is that the things which grew on trees here were surprisingly more appetite stimulating than anything back home. Back home at The Trinity, I found almost everything to be pretty bland. Maybe because the flavors back home were commonplace at this point. Maybe it's because these 5118208 flavors were so foreign, so exotic to my taste buds.

I was roaming in the dense forest at a considerable

distance from our landing site. It has been approximately a year and five months since we first landed here on 5118208. The research team has conducted countless experimentations here and has successfully synchronized all data with the central monitoring system back at the Venture-88. The continuous synchronization of the data has allowed us to produce immediate results that so far seemed promising.

The only problem was that the genetically modified organisms were still drastically affected by the temperature and the atmospheric pressure. The Animalia species residing on 5118208 had tough rugged skin, which meant these factors did not affect them as much as it did the organisms My mission here was to directly report back to The Elders about the effects of 5118208`s environment on the sustainability of genetically modified organisms so that they can function in a systematic way. *Systematic*, everything is always systematic in my world. Nothing is *spontaneous*, and 5118208 feels spontaneous. Everything grows here at a natural pace; I have seen it. The Animalia that I have encountered near our campsite are subjected to a timeline. At a certain age or time, they are no longer capable of sustaining life and just cease to exist. I remembered that it is actually referred to as *dying*. It must make life seem that much more… important.

Nothing dies at The Trinity. Everything, including the trees and the Animalia, are as long-living as us. I pluck an extravagant-looking flower from the nearby branch. The beauty of the blend of bright colors in each petal is exotic and hypnotizing. Why is it that everything here *feels* so much — yes exactly, it *feels* here, way more than it ever does back home. Strange indeed. I inhale the sweet scent of the flower and as soon as I take another step, my communicator starts to beep, indicating that I am stepping out of the safe zone. I sigh with disappointment. I have never been able to go any further than this. The Command Center had guided us to set a safe zone to avoid any potential casualties. I take a step back and immediately pause as my hand meets the yellow rays of the sun. I could not feel the warmth of the yellow sun. Before carrying out expeditions to planets having even the slightest difference in atmosphere from The Trinity, the crew is injected with adaptable Nanites which adjust the body of the crew according to the environment of each planet. That is why I could not feel the heat from the sun, which was a misfortune because I really wanted to know what it felt like. Since coming to 5118208, I am thoroughly surprised by my need of wanting to *feel* more rather than *assess*.

I pull my hand back and start on my way back to the excavation site. I was nearly out of the way of giant flapping leaves when I heard someone talking. My instinct told me to stay put because it is not considered decent to walk in on other people's conversations. I stood there so they could finish, however they were quite audible from where I was firmly positioned.

"…yes, I do not understand the logic of sending someone as inexperienced as Ms Tuloriah for an exploration as complex as this," I hear someone say, but I do not react immediately when I hear my name. Our kind is not one which indulges in unnecessary interactions, especially if it is about someone else. There is always logic in what we discuss and why we discuss it. I could not see who was talking, and neither was I interested in knowing.

"I agree, someone more experienced could have been appointed for the position but one cannot overlook Ms Tuloriah's incredible affinity for genetic science. I hear she *is* exceptional."

The other person says, "Agreed, maybe she is the kind which The Elders find special and decide to nurture into something great. I learned she was also good with Specie Psychology." The two members move away from where I could hear them, but I remain immovable. *Special*, a word I was awfully familiar with. This is the word my parents used to call me whenever I would excel at something. Even The Elders have appreciated my work and determination, but I did not find myself anything even remotely close to being special. There were far more superior beings present on The Trinity than me, but then why was I constantly being associated with this trait? I wonder if that is because there is no record of my biological parents and I was simply 'assigned' to my current parents. I was of the belief that people are only told they are special so they can believe they can do things they otherwise would never think to be possible. That we are all the same, with the potential to be so called 'special' in their own way. The exception being the Elders of course; they developed their extraordinary abilities through many aeons of being and learning.

I was deep in thought when my coms go off, *"Ms Tuloriah can you please report back to the laboratory?"* my assistant researcher says.

"I'm on my way," I reply.

I go through a quick sanitization cycle before entering into a white space, which is our temporary experimental laboratory. Here, we have engineered genetically modified life forms with the help of an artificially induced environment by using 5118208's atmosphere. Over the course of our year and five months, we have exposed the life forms to as many variations of the 5118208's atmosphere as possible. Since it is impossible that the climate of a certain planet remains constant for longer periods (unless it is engineered), we had to experiment with all possible climatic outcomes that may occur on the planet for at least another hundred years.

"Ms Tuloriah, the subjects are finally sustaining to variable temperature and pressure units and are even showing compatibility with the growth mechanism," the assistant researcher informs me with great positivity, while I gesture my hands for the 3D holographic images to start showing me the data. It was true, the data was correctly aligned and had been verified by the algorithm running the data from the Command Center. This was incredible! I did not anticipate that the results would start showing up this early. The verification from the central algorithm was proof that the findings were authentic.

"Ms Tuloriah, with results like these, we can even conclude the expedition before the predicted time!" the assistant researcher concludes appreciatively. Even I was having this determined *feeling* inside of me. I had done a fair amount of research, but never have I ever received such promising results, especially on site. I punch in numbers on the holographic images and command the AI to patch me through to the Command Center. I had to log in this information for the captain so he could provide us with further instructions.

"Commencing communication channel with Command Center," the AI announces. After a few seconds, the holographic image of the captain appears. "Greetings Ms Tuloriah," the captain says.

"To you too, Captain. I believe you have assessed the data?" I say almost too quickly.

The captain clears his throat and nods in agreement, "Yes Ms Tuloriah, and I must congratulate you on the desirable results."

I finally muster a smile. I somehow feel quite appreciated.

"Please be advised that your arrival at Venture-88

would initiate from the start of the next Sol month. The main Research Center at The Trinity believes that the data is accurate enough to conclude this expedition as successful."

"Roger that, Captain," I reply with a slight twitch of my mouth to show that I am pleased with his orders.

"Once we reach The Trinity, you will be obliged to present your findings to the Council and then receive an official verdict regarding your expedition," the captain further informs me.

"Acknowledged, Captain!" I reply shortly, and the hologram disappears.

Later that day, we receive a memo to conclude our findings so that the AI can run the algorithm for one final verification. It was strange; when you are so passionately looking forward to something, the rotation of planets, tends to go by quicker than usual. Before the day of our departure, I set out to the forest to see the magnificence of 5118208 for a final time. It was almost hilarious that the planet I was dreading to come to would grow on me to such an extent, but it was rather lonely here. And no one wants to leave their home, no matter how systematic and allocated I found The Trinity. Regardless, it was still home, and my family was there. I might like to come back to 5118208 someday, but for now, this much time on this planet seemed enough to leave me content.

I walk to the edge of the safe zone to find a good spot for what I held in my hands. I find a good damp spot and the soil seemed steady as well. I dig the soil with my bare hands, until I make a small cup in the ground. I use the retinal scanner on the box I was carrying to open it. Carefully, I place the box on the ground and remove its contents. I place the little stalk of the Hemploid plant in the little cup I had dug. I carefully merge the tiny roots of the baby plant with the soil and throw the dirt back in. I smooth over the ground and stand up with the box. *A tiny gift,* I say to myself and then I say to the little plant, "You may not have the same properties here as you have on The Trinity because of the difference of ecologies, but you'll still do wonders here as well." I gently pat the baby plant and head back to the excavation site.

"Command Center, we are a go for launch. Please be advised on the launch and docking velocity," the pilot informs the Command Center and punches in the variables for the velocity. Our mission was ending, and we were all set to go home. The ride back to Venture-88 was uneventful, but as we crossed the threshold into the nothingness of space, I really started to miss the vibrancy of the planet; the incredible colors, the energy and especially the nature. As I look out the window, I can see the little patches of green and blue becoming a speck as our ship ascends towards Venture-88. *Spertik was right,* I thought, *it was a life-changing experience.*

Back at the Venture, the crew formally congratulates us on our success and the captain is more than pleased with our efforts. The captain shakes my hand and says, "Great work Ms Tuloriah, this was something special." Again, with the word special. I was still undecided about how I felt about the word special being used for me or my activities. I politely respond to everyone's greetings, and then quickly confine myself to my cabin to prepare for my hibernation pod. It was a long journey back and I feel I wanted to hop in my hibernation pod as quickly as I could. Again, I *feel*. I really need to take time and study the effects of planetary ecology on specie psychology, because I was starting to feel the difference in my demeanor But I planned to deal with that once I reached The Trinity.

I lay back in the hibernation pod and let the familiar sense of calm take over as the hatch closes on top of me. My eyes close with it as well.

I feel the air rush back into my lungs again, and I feel the familiar warmth of the blood rushing inside me. The hatch of the hibernation pod dislodges, indicating that the ship will be arriving at its destination soon.

"All personnel stand by for landing safety protocols. Ship docking in T — minus ten minutes." The announcement is made on the coms, and I feel quite relieved. I go through the compulsory sanitation process and put my uniform on to assemble in the ship's docking bay. All of the Academy would be waiting for us, not to mention that all the researchers from the Technological Advancement facility will be there as well. The captain stands at the front, with all the crew members standing in queues behind him in the order of their rank. We hear

the booming sound of the large ship docking in the hangar and as soon as we land, the bay door opens. I sense the familiar air of home. We march outside the ship in an orderly fashion, walking between paths with tons of people waving at us from all sides. They were all there to congratulate us.

Soon after we arrived, I was instructed to appear before the Council for my debriefing. I walk the familiar path to the Great Hall, like I first did when I was chosen to go to 5118208. But the incentive has changed now, as has the future prospect. I enter into the glory of the Great Hall, where the Council awaits me. I greet the Elders with utmost respect, and they pay it back.

"Ms Tuloriah, we must first convey our deepest gratitude for the services you have provided for the greater good of our specie," one of the Elders addresses me, continuing, "we would like to hear the core findings from you Ms Tuloriah." I nod.

"I would like to make an assertion here in front of the great Council with a profound positivity that the mission has been a success. The genetically engineered organisms have successfully developed an adaptable mechanism which corresponds well to the variation in temperature, pressure and even the radiation from the sun. However, these experiments were conducted in a very controlled and delicate environment, because the 5118208's ecology is still very harsh for these organisms or life forms to survive on their own. Furthermore, the Animalia species which are dominant on 5118208 right now are incredibly hostile and the limited evolution of our life forms will not last with them still roaming around."

When I finished my briefing, there was a long pause until one of the Elders spoke in a grave tone, "Ms Tuloriah, what is your suggestion on how to utilize our resources enough for these primitive life forms to survive?"

"If we carefully examine the data, then hypothetically speaking, 5118208 would need to undergo an extensive series of planetary level terraforming in order to fully sustain the genetically modified life forms" There was a silence in the Great Hall, which I would describe surprisingly as awkward because it was beyond my intelligence to apprehend what was going on in the minds of the Elders.

"Ms Tuloriah, is terraforming 5118208 to support the engineered life forms possible?"

I nod in answer to the query of the Elder.

"Of course it can, but the terraforming would require a series of catalytic reactions for a planet like 5118208. The process would need a catastrophic amount of gravitational impact which would modify the ecosystem," I reply, and after a pause further add, "however that would mean mass level extinction of the existing species." I inferred this would seem like a concerning point for the Elders since our specie does not stand for voluntary genocide of any other species, especially if it were for our own interests. However, the silence of the Elders was speaking for something else. After several minutes, I was gestured to exit the Great Hall, which I did. However, I was anxious as to what they would conclude with what I had briefed them about. I was in deep thought about what it could possibly be that the Council was interested in, when clearly, they cannot do anything worthwhile without terraforming 5118208.

I push my thoughts aside because it was not my place to question the decisions of the Council. Later that day, I request to arrange transportation to meet my family. It has been twenty years since I have been able to see them, but then again time here is irrelevant. If it had been thirty years even, they would not have felt it to be long because that is how it is here. When you have lived for hundreds and thousands of years, you tend to misplace the importance of extended farewells; for them, it must have felt like a few days. Nonetheless, I was finally home, and my work was done. Now, I could use the company of my family and invest my time towards studying the psychological effects that 5118208 had had on me, though it was an experience which I will always remember in a positive light. Although, I have a sinking feeling this mission is not truly over.

Chapter 4
Execution

My suspicions proved to be true. I had to join the scouts for research, again. I was not to question the Elders' decision and if they wanted me there, I had to join the team. We had to revisit 5118208 with a mission of collecting additional samples with the objective of cultivation, extending our own species on yet another planet. The Elders had decided to begin the humanoid integration and inhabitation process. And I was to be the model sample for splicing. With their objectives now known, this made this mission back to 5118208 all the more daunting.

This was not my first visit, but this time I was caught in the middle of acceptance and denial. The 5118208 was to be my home for now and though it seemed like a dead place, I still had to bring it to life. We were here to collect specimens, to cultivate and in the process, there was a possibility of me discovering what this planet meant to me and my purpose. It was clear to me the connection I've come realize I have with this place, and I still wanted to know why.

I had left the place with intentions of not returning as I thought this place required a lot of organic development. Though it was possible, as I informed the Elders, I still lacked the motivation. Even though I still hadn't found any I wasn't left with many options but to force myself to research in a proper manner. This was to be my home. I was satisfied living in The Trinity. The home is a place where a person acquires peace. It is a place where you get a sense of belonging and no matter how imperfect your residence might be, it is yours and that ownership is sufficient. That was my idea of home; however, the Elders thought differently. They were looking for a life cycle that had an end, unlike ours. They had their reasons and I had mine. There was no point of debate as I knew the Elders had a deeper understanding of the eco-system and what was required to create a substantial level of life. I was home, away from home.

Everything on this planet seemed different. The sun from down here looked awfully small. The stars seemed to be even smaller. There was a wide range of plants and their varieties were indeed beautiful. When I first came here, I was a visitor. I was amused by every little thing that I looked at, but because this time I was there on a mission which was to make it a place we were never to return from, my amusement had reduced. It's not that the plants were no more attractive, but my mind in slight unknown frustration wanted me to find things which were less attractive. I was looking for the oddities.

The Animalia specie and the plantae species here were very different from The Trinity. Every specie was very unique from the other. There were animals that were very huge and then there were others who were so small that they couldn't be seen from a meter's distance. They were in every color and had different sizes and shapes. Each plant was unique from the other, too. Some were dry and hard while some were soft. Some had edibles of different sizes and shapes, while others seemed treacherous and forbidden. I hadn't been here long, but it seemed very much like I had. The time on 5118208 was very short. It would be bright for some time and then it would get dark and that too not for long. Days were passing by so quickly that it seemed like I had been here for a considerably long time. I had calculated the difference in time periodicity between 5118208 and The Trinity. So, I knew what the reason was.

Through this time, I was in contact with the Elders. I had the Satophone which allowed us to communicate with the Elders from different planets and galaxies. I would contact them after eleven transformations of the sky from bright to dark. The Elders never reacted much. Instead, they listened closely and remained calm.

We were first sent to look for more options besides the 5118208. And surfing through the entire galaxy, there was no other place that was as appropriate as the 5118208 was. We visited the Ceres. It was only rock and ice there. There weren't any species there and it was the heaviest planet of the asteroid belt. We visited the Charon. It was small and the weather conditions were very discouraging. There were 40 billion planets we were searching from and out of all the others, 5118208 was undoubtedly the best fit for our mission. We searched through various asteroid belts but were unable to find a planet, other than 5118208, having the size, shape and environment to our satisfaction.

The samples were to be collected of every plant and animal species that existed. I accompanied the other scouts who were designated the task. We needed their samples so we could generate an asteroid that was perfectly suitable for the conditions of the 5118208. The poles of the 5118208 were very cold and the center extremely hot. The animals and plants living in those places had suitable skin and features which allowed them to survive. Humanoids are a kind of specie that can't be restricted and the intention of The Elders was to extend our own kind to live finitely on this planet. The microorganisms which were to grow and populate the humanoid species required a fair bit of everything. There was a balance to be created which permitted them to live in different conditions, adopt and most importantly inhabit without being limited to any particular region due to weather or other natural factors.

The council had sent me there to deeply explore every living specie. It wasn't an easy task. There were millions of Animalia and Plantae species there and to get samples of each and every one was going to be very difficult. The species were unique based on their geographical location. I knew it because my father had told me about how the species existed on this planet on our last expedition together. It was difficult to find all the land species and that there were more animals and plants that lived underground. There were millions under water.

I had discussed with the Elders that it was going to be very challenging and despite their insistence to get a sample of every single one, I knew they would understand. The Council wanted this deeper research mission to be fruitful leading to positive results. I decided to categorize our sample collection based on geographical divisions. We wanted to create microorganisms which had the tendency to live in different conditions. If we were able to get samples of species living in different regions, the chances of creating a perfect microbe were maximum. The plan seemed sound, but the council was to be convinced for approval. I decided to setup my Satophone and discuss it with the Elders. Though we were millions of miles apart, the Satophone allowed us to connect in no time. I would request them for contact, and then they would connect with me through the device at the time they scheduled.

***

"This is second time you are there without your father Ms Tuloriah, we are confident you will do fine, just as he did," said one of the Elders from the Council.

It was a hint of being indirectly advised to do the task as ordered without requesting for any alterations in the plan.

"I will not let you down" I reply.

"Anything of immediate concern, Ms Tuloriah? There aren't many days left and I expect things are going according to the plan?" Another member spoke cementing my perception that they were not in any mood for discussions.

I take a deep breath and start to explain: *"It will take a lot of time to look for every specie, I'm not saying that it isn't possible—"*

I'm interrupted. *"If it isn't, then do it!"*

I continue, *"All I'm saying is that we should divide our research team into members who collect a sufficient number of samples from different geographical locations as different locations have different conditions which satisfy our cause. The purpose of the advice is to escalate the process and not derail it."*

This time the Council listened to what I had to say and since I made sense, they did not write off my suggestion straight away.

"Will it then be done in the time you've been given?" the head of the Council asks. There was a long pause before he spoke. I could feel my opinion being valued. If the head of the Council gets convinced, the rest will most probably follow.

"Yes, it should be if I'm permitted from now," I reply in a confident tone. The tone indicated I had

confidence in my plans and was willing to take responsibility for it.

"Get it done your way. Make sure, Ms Tuloriah, that our ultimate goal is not risked in the process. I know you will return with the ideal samples." The head of the Council of Elders finally allowed me to go through with my plans. I was not certain that I would be able to convince them, but I suppose because of the kind of reputation I had and the logic I explained with I was successful in doing so. The connection suddenly terminated.

***

I got the approval I needed but the job had just begun. We were to gather information on different species, and the limit of the variety for each location was set to 500. There were twelve days remaining and since we hadn't planned the research earlier, the data we had was difficult to be categorized on that basis as it wasn't gathered on that approach. Nevertheless, twelve days are what we had at hand, and they were enough if the collection phase was taken care of smartly.

I was involved in the research process which made me feel I was digging a hole for myself. If the sample collection strategy turned out to be beneficial, which it was to be as per my analysis, there was a possibility that I might be asked to live here, permanently. I would have to live away from my family and home. I had to be away from The Trinity. I did not know what was coming my way, but I had to embrace whatever it was to be. I did not want to think much about it as it was only to decrease my productivity toward the research.

I wasn't the only scout who had such concerns. It was a discussion amongst most of the scouts to whether they would be deployed to live on this planet and have to give up on their families. It's not that they were never to revisit their loved ones, but the time the deployed scouts were to live away was indefinite.

"Ms Tuloriah, we were all discussing who are the ones who are most likely to stay here and do you know what most of us think?" one of the scouts says. I was listening very closely to him. I knew where he was going with it but because I was so involved in my thoughts, I only nodded hoping it would lead to somewhere other than my expectation.

"Most of us think you will," he says, smiling at me. I was to be here whether alone or accompanied, and everyone knew it, including myself. I smiled back at him. There was nothing I had in my defense. He had a point, and I was secretly scared of it turning into reality.

"You are a tough champ Ms Tuloriah, you'll do fine." He ends the conversation I was never verbally part of. He reminds me that closing my eyes on reality would not take me away from it. I knew what he said made perfect sense, but the other thing I realized was that they looked up to me. They all thought of me as somebody who was most capable of settling down in a

57

different environment, adapting. I did not question my capabilities and I too had confidence that I was capable of carrying out the entire process. It was love that held me back. I had a family, a home, people who I wanted to be around. It's not that I wasn't willing to give them up for the greater good of our kind, I just was holding on to the little bit of hope that it would not be asked of me.

Whether or not I was to live a nomadic life on 5118208, I had to get the samples to fulfill my promise that I made to the Elders, so I rejoined the team which was looking for the asteroids with the various galaxies. Searching from place to place exploring around in the Baptistina family we finally came across something significant. There were two teams of scouts sent from The Trinity. One of them was directly sent to 5118208, while the other went to find another planet that was as good as the 5118208. Later when no planet proved to be as good as 5118208, I was sent here as I had been to 5118208 with my father before. My past journey indicated that I could collect the right samples too.

The other team had been looking for asteroids and collecting samples but since their exploration was planned to be a detailed one, there was a great part of the galaxy they hadn't explored. The asteroids of the Baptistina family were least explored. I knew if I could find the Chicxulub asteroid, all our problems were to be solved. My father had recounted his encounter with it many travels ago. It was a loner for a time, traveling through the universe as if searching for its purpose. The last known coordinates were entered into our trajectory indicator to locate its potential location. The team found it in a remarkable amount of time. I was sent to examine its mission potential. When I arrived at its location, the asteroid was being held in a holding pattern by our ship. I was amused to see it as there was nothing similar to it in the other parts of the universe. As I got closer, I realized it was indeed very different.

It was impossible to carry the complete asteroid and neither did I even think of it. The right samples were sufficient to extract out what we were looking for. We collected the samples and loaded them in our spaceship to return home. We were well prepared and had all the necessary equipment to get them safely to Trinity. The research mission was to be called off as we had discovered the most essential asteroid. I secretly felt proud of myself. I had kept my promise as I was returning with probably the solution to all our problems

***

I was called by the Council to brief them about my expedition. The Elders knew I was returning with something substantial as I called it off sooner than later. Though the Elders never said this directly, I felt they had a lot of expectations associated with me. I was internally very happy to have been able to recover the Chicxulub asteroid, which could lead to inhabiting the

5118208.

The moment I reached the Council, there was no more need for briefing about the project. They were all smiling, proud of the way I had lived up to their expectations. This certainly did increase my chances to be sent back again, but in that moment, I really did not want to think about anything else other than the success of our mission. 5118208 was undisputedly the most ideal planet when compared to billions of others in the galaxy, and the recovery of the asteroid had confirmed it to be the right choice. My trust in the Elders solidified. They indeed knew about 5118208, which is why all their focus was on this planet and not looking for others.

Chapter 5
Count Down

It was time to take things a step further. We had successfully executed the first phase of the plan, but the next phase was going to be way more complex and challenging. When I was out collecting samples, I had confidence in the plan but secretly wished against it because I knew what this would lead to. Even then, I never compromised the mission nor reduced my efforts. That's how I was programmed to be, obedient and compelling.

The next step was to place the micro-organisms in the asteroid. They were to be smartly distributed. There was a risk that if they weren't placed in the right parts of the asteroid, the whole mission would have been at stake. It was not going to be easy to re-collect those samples and re-process the entire matching procedure.

The bigger risk was the survival of the micro-organisms They were designed to grow in sheltered and regulated conditions. If the environment they were placed in was not balanced, they were much less likely to not make it through and the whole mission would fail in its initial stages. The micro-organisms were synthesized a great deal but were yet to be experimented on real grounds.

The scouts were not responsible for the formation of the micro-organisms. They were simply not capable of doing it. The micro-organisms were prepared by the Elders. The core ingredients were two acids prepared by them, which were ribonucleic acid and de-ox ribonucleic acid. The genetic material was present to evolve with time being adaptable to its surroundings and grow accordingly. For it to provide energy, they had created the mitochondria which were to grasp energy from the environment. They had engineered microbes that balanced the overall biological structure of these organisms, which were about to gradually take their predicted size and shape if they were placed in the correct locations.

The surreal beings had been living on this planet for aeons. They had a different understanding of this entire concept. They were not amused by the idea of entering into its executional steps one after another, but they rather questioned the entire plan. Why was there a need for another planet? What void were these micro-organisms intended to fill? The micro-organisms did not have the potential or traits of the surreal beings. They were created to be different, to have a different cycle, to experience death and perish in short spans, unlike the surreal beings.

The concept of a new planet was perceived differently by everyone. But most of the surreal beings were not really impressed by it. Though the physical features of the micro-organisms formed by the Elders were different from the surreal beings including their visual and audible capacities, the thinking parameters were designed of the same complexity. The question still remained as to why this had to happen.

The Elders had made all the necessary preparations and calculations, which were required to execute the next phase of placement. Their process seemed to be delaying for apparently no solid reason. The Elders were aware of the speculations and discussions between the surreal beings. They were considering their reservations and thinking over them before finally executing as per the plan. They, along with the scout leader, were convinced that there was nothing wrong with the concept. The scout leader had witnessed different parts of the universe and knew the potential this Milky Way had over the others. It was definitely worth a try, which is why the scout leader approached the Elders to place his point. He encouraged them that there was nothing wrong with their approach. The plan was initiated after considering all the aspects associated with it. He encouraged them to proceed without further considerations as the rest was all dependent on experimentation and they had control over terminating the process whenever they felt it was not what they were looking for.

It was not a very simple conversation as the pros and cons were possibly way more than expected. However, the scout leader believed that if they had made it this far in this plan, continuing it was the wisest thing to do. The Elders agreed.

The surreal beings had different reservations when compared to mine. They were concerned about the existence of other living things and their impact on the organisms living on The Trinity. I, on the other hand, did not want to leave my family. The way it was progressing, the chances of me being on the other planet as a caretaker were only increasing. Even if I weren't there to be the caretaker, I was certain the Elders would have thought of some job for me related to the project. I was only hoping that the duty to be assigned to me was something I could perform while living with my family on The Trinity. I knew this wasn't going to be the case, but I needed something to look to; in this situation, it was hope.

Experimentation and discoveries always excited me. I got this from my father as he spent most of his life trying to explore new possibilities and practiced his theories in an attempt to justify them and even worked for their further simplification. It was because of him that the Chicxulub asteroid was selected amongst the other options, as he was the one who first indicated that micro-organisms could be synthetically produced and could inhabit the specific part of the universe where they were now being placed.

I knew he was doing it for a reason. He had a vision which supported the theories he formulated, though a lot of it had gone away with him and the Elders were the only ones who knew most about him. I was proud of his vision and efforts but had no clue that being his daughter all the responsibility was to be transferred on to me. I was not afraid of taking responsibility, but the problem lied in the compromise I had to make to ensure that the operations were carried out as per schedule and the objectives set were achieved.

I was happy that I was able to contribute to my father's mission, but in no way did I imagine that the contribution I was making was going to take me away from my life in its entirely. By the time I had realized this would be my life, I did not have many options. Well, I never had the option; if the Elders would have asked me to execute the task under any circumstances, I was not to question them.

I wanted to prepare myself mentally but was unable to do so. Initially, I believed I had ample time to redirect my mindset, and with the passage of time I would be comfortable to move to another planet, but time had no mercy on me. The more the time passed by, the more it drew me closer to leaving my family and I was less motivated to do so.

It seemed funny to me as if I were paving the path for my own departure. The Trinity was not going to be as exciting as the chosen planet was going to be. I was going to witness transformation there. Something that, as a scout, I could only have dreamed of, but then again, what flavor was the dream to have if it missed the ingredients of love and companionship?

I am a goal-oriented person; the fellow beings told me that's exactly how my father was. I was focused on complying to the task at hand with complete determination and all my personal needs were secondary unless they were in context to the stake of my survival. The Elders knew that even though I did not want to leave, if I were made to, I would not disappoint them. It puzzled me as I was unable to distinguish it being my strength or a weakness.

I liked the planet. It had a sense of uniqueness attached to it. I loved how the waterfalls looked from a fair distance. How the mountains stood on the 5118208 seemingly helping it hold up his shape. The snowflakes on the extreme corners of this planet seemed mesmerizing. There were quite a few things that fascinated me. I loved being there, but the question was for how long was I going to enjoy those pleasing sights?

I had to break the news to my family, especially Lharkin. I had given them an idea, and despite the fact that I wasn't completely sure, I considered it to be unfair to them all if they were informed in the very last moments. I also kept in mind that maybe the Elders changed their decision of executing the plan. There was also a slight possibility that they might choose some other scout for the job. If that were to happen, breaking the news to my Lharkin and my parents would only depress them just the way it depressed me. Since the probabilities were against my will, I decided to discuss it with Lharkin.

I was already undergoing a lot of mental struggle, to digest it myself and in this situation, convincing him was going to be even more difficult. I needed convincing myself, but that's what family is there for, I believe. To share the joys and sorrows and find the support that otherwise might be non-existent.

I found an opportunity and told him I wanted to talk about something. He already knew something was wrong. Before I even started telling him what was bothering me, he already said he had noticed me not being comfortable in the last few days. He was hoping for it to settle down because he did not want to see me so worried any more. He knew me so well. His concern made me weaker; I thought of not telling him and diverting it to something else, but I had made up my mind. I had assessed all the factors and realized that if I hadn't told him, it would be more difficult for him to deal with.

Maybe this was an attempt by me of helping myself. I told him about the aftereffects of the mission. He heard me without any haste and did not react until I was finished. I was expecting a different reaction from him. I thought he would fight with me or lose his control when I gave him the news, but his reaction was completely different. It's not that I wanted him to react that way, in fact, that reaction would have been even more difficult for me to handle.

He did not lose his composure the entire time. It was like somebody was allowing me to breathe it all out, all of it. As I sat there, looking into his eyes, I could see he was trying his best to hold back his emotional responses. He wanted to be there for me. I told him how difficult it was for me to tell him, let alone leave him behind before we could truly explore the depths of our coupling. I could see his vulnerability, which was evident from his eyes, but not his words. He hugged me without saying another word and we sat in that position for the next fifteen minutes. It seemed like we remained that way for a couple of Julian years.

He then sat back and started by telling me how much he loved me. I felt weaker. His words were so powerful that they went right through my mind into my soul. I was glad to have a life partner like him. When he told me that he loved me, I was surprised as we always had worked closely together on missions without so much of a conversation of a potential coupling. He knew if the Elders had chosen me, there was a reason behind it.

He then told me how proud he was of me. I had accomplished what many of the other scouts could not. I was not the only one out there trying to get the right samples, but I was the only one successful in bringing what the Elders had asked for. He related my efforts to praise my father's research and told me that my father would have been very proud of me. Every word coming out of his mouth was guiding me in the direction of patience and control. Every word was consoling.

He held my hands, kissed them and lifted them to

his tear-filled eyes. I was unable to hold my tears. I was satisfied by telling him about my long and probably never-ending journey. The way he handled me, I am quite sure nobody else could have. He reminded me of the times of first meeting, our first mission together. It was like he was giving me a flashback of all the times we had spent together. One after another, he walked me through our entire journey.

The battle which had been going inside of me after the placement of the micro-organisms finally seemed to get under control. He was gradually pulling me out of my anxiety and replacing the weakness caused by the memories we shared to strengths. At that moment, I did not know the impression it was casting on me, but it all felt so relieving that I did not focus on anything else but on the transmission of his honest emotions into my soul.

He told me that just like my father, my family would also be proud of me when they realized why I left them. He said the respect I had earned was not comparable. I was not doing anything for myself, but for my fellow beings and that was something no one besides a person of great honor could do. I knew he meant everything he was saying. He wasn't trying to console me but was just being honest and transparent about how he felt and thought of me.

He made me understand that there are not a lot of people who stand up for others, struggle for others, or continue to fulfill the dreams of their loved ones. I was one of them. I suddenly started feeling reassured of all I was chosen to do. I was so overridden by the love of family that I had overlooked the impact of the sacrifice I was making.

I went through an internal transformation where I was in the middle of acceptance and denial. I had mixed emotions as I was achieving and losing at the same time. He convinced me that the achievement was by far greater than the loss. He made me think of it in a different dimension and I could only agree to everything he said.

I asked him how I was to react to difficult situations without him. When I felt lonely or had to make difficult decisions, he was not going to be by my side, who was to help me then? He assured me that he knew I was capable of finding a way out of every situation. As I looked into his rainbow, star-like eyes, I smiled, seeing all the reasons why he was my soul's mirror.

"Think about me Tuloriah, when you feel weak or confused, I wish to be your strength. A strength that is not dependent on my presence, but my love," he said to me.

These words were sufficient for me to take on anything. I had finally gained solitude. I was certain that the idea of moving to planet 5118208 was not that bad after all. This was not something that was for my own well-being, but everyone else who lived in The Trinity. There were still a lot of questions unanswered, but they did not matter any more.

I knew it was going to be very difficult to live without him. I knew it was going to be challenging, but the mental preparations I had long waited for, were achieved. I was ready for any decision the Elders made. I was willing to shift to that planet for an uncertain length of time. I was determined to fulfill my father's dream. I hoped that I was going to get a chance to visit my family more often than not. I knew the Elders had the best of plans. I had forgotten it and I can only thank my Lharkin for reminding me. I was ready for a new beginning, which was no more than something my family was excluded from; it was only their physical absence. I knew I was the best scout for the job and I finally found the motivation I thought I would never find.

It was a mission that was to last for a lifetime. It was the beginning of a new dimension of my life. I had to look forward to moving ahead. I had set my mind straight and was convinced to start on this never-ending journey.

Chapter 6
Bang

It was time to launch the asteroid. All the necessary preparations had been made. The people of Trinity were excited to see how it worked while the Elders were confident that the results would be in line with their predictions.

A team was prepared that consisted of mostly members of the research team. The purpose of the team was to monitor the entire process and update the Elders on how it was proceeding. I was assigned to head the team.

The time had come, and the asteroid was launched from our solar system. They were fascinating visuals. As soon as the asteroid left our solar system, it took it over fifteen days to land on 5118208. Even though it could have hit the 5118208 in a shorter period, it was rerouted to balance out the impact. If it were headed on the shortest path, there was a possibility that it could destroy the entire planet 5118208.

The spaceship had twenty-eight members on it including me. It was a huge ship that had provision for over 72 solar days, since 72 days were enough to conclude if the venture was or was not successful.

Further provisions were then to be provided later if the execution went as planned. There were twelve rooms in the spaceship. Nine rooms were for the twenty-seven members that included ship maintenance staff and inter-planet communication specialists. One room was for the commanding officer of the ship, I had that room. The other two rooms were for other domestic purposes.

The day the ship was to leave was one day prior to the launch. The ship was to be placed in a position in between the 5118208 and The Trinity. It was to be in a middle position from where both the asteroids launched, and its impact could be precisely monitored. All the members that were selected to board the ship were the best research and analytical specialists. I had a great team working with me. However, they were all supposed to leave Trinity forever. I was one out of the twenty-eight who was sent off, never to return. The only way I was to return was if the mission failed. I couldn't have prayed for it to fail nor was I able to hope for it to be successful. It was quite a dilemma.

The launching pad that was to eject the asteroid was the largest of the five we had at Trinity. While leaving I had mixed feelings of surrender and achievement simultaneously battling inside of me. The people of Trinity were very excited to see it happen. Huge crowds had gathered to witness its release whereas, we were at the spaceship where all we got was news from Trinity. *It was going to be this way forever now, at least for me*, I thought to myself.

It was only a matter of days the ship needed to reach its desired spot, and so it did. We were given a signal prior to the launching and we had the monitors of our screen showing us visuals of the launch. As soon as the asteroid was ejected, it left Trinity in a flash and as soon as it entered space, it slowed down. For a moment there was chaos. The landing of the asteroid on its programmed target seemed to be very unlikely as its speed was decreasing at a very rapid pace. It turned out that one of the engines out of the nineteen engines installed in it to carry it through space to 5118208 had shut down. Just when it seemed like the mission had failed in its initial phases, the engine restarted and everybody on the spaceship sighed with relief; most probably the Elders did too.

It had been seven days and the asteroid that had the location sensor inserted in showed signs of it heading in the right direction. Everyone on Trinity and the spaceship was eagerly waiting for the time to complete and see the results. My crew members were just as nervous as I was.

The screen showed amazing images when the asteroid left Trinity. The engines sparked an orange flame, which was so intense that the asteroid could barely be seen. It seemed as though the asteroid was surrounded by fog and could only be clearly seen once it was at a fair distance from Trinity. More specifically, only the red lights attached in the topmost corner of the asteroid could be seen. The purpose of the lights was to identify the asteroid even in places where the absence of light and other space force was immaculate.

The asteroid hit the 5118208 in the place now called Mexico. The images were even more mesmerizing. If the asteroid had crashed any place besides where it did, then the unwanted species would have survived, and the complexities of the plan would only have increased. We had never been this particular about the demographics of 5118208 before. The terraforming indicated that it was indeed something huge. None of us could have predicted to see the sights that depicted different colors beneath which the 5118208 was transforming and changing into a place that was going to be suitable for civilization to begin. The colors on display were because of different reactions caused by the heat, which had resulted due to the crash.

The dinosaurs that were abundant of the species had to be removed to make 5118208 a suitable place. It was about changing the dynamics of 5118208 and the species living there. It was making the condition of the 5118208 more suitable for different species that included the creation of the most sophisticated species that were similar to us in shape and functionality but were of shorter lifespans and more limited powers.

The dinosaurs were mostly present in the part of the 5118208 now called South America. It was time for the species of the dinosaurs to go extinct. All dinosaurs, no matter what size and shape, were turning to dust. The communication team, consisting of seven members, was dedicated to reporting to the Elders. They had updated the Elders of the fact that the landing was perfect, and the next update was the most important of all. They had to tell the Elders that all the species that were to be eliminated were, in fact, eliminated as per the plan. The way things progressed, it was only a matter of time before we were to give the Elders a heads up that the execution was perfect and that the mission was a success.

Millions and millions of species went extinct. The species included various animals and plants, all of which made the living conditions difficult for new species to come into existence. They weren't just land species but the impact was so huge that even some of the unwanted water species were to turn into dust and so they did. It was only a matter of few seconds and the picture of the 5118208 had completely transformed in accordance with our calculations.

While everybody in the spaceship was impressed by seeing extraordinary images, I stood there thinking about my life back home. I wondered what Lharkin would be doing then. I was missing everyone and tears streamed down my cheek as I thought of them all. One of my companions on the spaceship asked why I had tears streaming down my face and as I did not want to discuss my pain with anyone, I responded: "Are the images not amazing?"

Yes, the images were amazing, and none of us had

seen anything like it before, but for me it was more than just the beginning of a new civilization. It was life changing for me in which my physical self was to remain unchanged while a new mental character was to be developed. A mental character that did not consist of many emotions and was more focused than it used to be. It was the only way I could have survived the never-ending journey. A journey my father solely began which was now backed by the whole Trinity and I was the chosen one.

We had done the math and knew that once the asteroid crashed, its impact was to result in the release of a huge number of sulfurs and hydrocarbons. They were a necessity as the enormous amount of chemicals was to create a layer over the 5118208 after which the visibility from outside the 5118208 was going to be zero. The no-visibility phase had more to it. It was to block the sunlight. The blockage of the sunlight was to maintain a cool temperature that would allow the micro-organisms implanted in the asteroid to survive. If the climatic control were skipped, the hot temperature of the 5118208 would have made it impossible for the micro-organisms to thrive.

As the micro-organisms were handpicked after the detailed research process, losing them was not an option. There was a lot of effort we had put in and we couldn't have just let it all go away due to lack of research work and calculations.

It was then the turn of the task force to get close to

5118208 and drop the device through the sulfur and hydrocarbon layer in order to monitor how conditions were changing. The spaceship drew closer to the 5118208. But before the task force members could exit under my command, a meteoroid flying in the air sliced past the right wing, hitting it hard, which resulted in the spaceship started to lose its course. The greatest concern then was to ensure that we did not fall inside the layer on to the 5118208. This could have tampered with the layer and the collision had the potential of taking our lives. Luckily, the ship did not fall towards the 5118208, but away from it though it hadn't gained any stability yet.

We tried to ensure that the damage was controlled. We had a repairing mechanism that was auto controlled through the control center of the ship. We were successful in being able to repair the broken wing through the repair mechanism and now only the manual work was left, which was of refitting navigation devices that were destroyed by the collision. Five members jumped out including me and we planted the devices in their designated areas. We had survived.

The collision had generated a signal back to Trinity. The Elders immediately made contact to ensure we were fine. They wanted to speak with me in person in the meeting room. I told them there what had happened, and they were relieved to know that things were now under control. We were now to head back, hoping that no meteoroid would hit us this time. We were blinded by

5118208 conditions as we did not know whether the right temperature was maintained and if the conditions were suitable for the micro-organisms

We closed in and I along with two more partners stepped out to drop the devices through a shooting gun. We had the parameters set but were seven hundred kilometres away from the layer. The spaceship couldn't get closer to a distance of nine hundred kilometres as the gravitational pull could have pulled it down, resulting in the collision we were fighting to avoid.

It wasn't necessary for me to go out myself, but since I was the most experienced and skilled of the lot, I decided to take the responsibility myself. We closed in and were successfully able to shoot the devices. This was just the first round as then we had directed the devices in areas, which were closer to the asteroids. More devices were to be dropped down but across the entire planet, so we could monitor the uniformity of conditions and ensure survival at all the places of the 5118208.

We boarded back on the ship and now had to move to the other side of the planet. We did so and things went very smoothly there. The poles were the last targets of dropping devices. We moved first to the north side where we dropped it with ease, and the case of the south side was not very different. Once all the devices were dropped, we boarded back and took the spaceship back to its position, which was the middle point of The Trinity and the 5118208. The distance formed reflected an Isosceles triangle from where the 5118208 and Trinity were at equal distances.

When we started monitoring through the devices we had dropped, it turned out that the layer was too thick, and the conditions of the planet were getting very cold. Just as how extremely hot conditions were not good for the micro-organisms, neither were extremely cold ones.

I contacted the Elders and told them about the climatic problem. This wasn't something we were prepared for. Extreme cold conditions were not expected, and we did not have a counter plan. We had to make sure that the thickness of the layer was reduced in a way that it did not make such conditions too frequent. But how were we to alter its thickness anyway?

The Elders were also very concerned and suggested I do what I felt was right. "Find a solution, just the way your father would have."

Though they had provided me with the motivation, they hadn't given me any solution. I started thinking and looking for a solution. I wasn't sure how it was to happen.

I started thinking. I had to keep in mind the resources we had at hand and utilize them in order to satisfy our goals. I kept on thinking and thinking when suddenly an idea struck my mind. I figured we could use the fluorine cylinders we had stored on the ship for medical purposes. What fluorine would do was react with the hydrocarbons in the layer and reduce its thickness. But the problem that arose was that we lacked fluorine present at the ship and going back to Trinity to get more would cost a lot of time.

We used the fluorine cylinders we had and informed The Trinity to prepare for more cylinders. This helped us to buy some time. The elders sent off another spaceship that had only two members and tons of fluorine, which was ample for the process. Meanwhile, I did the calculations and gradually hit streams of fluorine at the layer in order for it to react and get thinner. We rechecked the results every eleven hours. Gladly the plan worked, and the climatic conditions balanced out. Now they weren't too hot nor were they too cold.

The Elders were glad of the results. They said they were very proud of how I handled the situation. They told me this is why they wanted me there and nobody else. I thought about how proud my father would have been seeing me controlling the chaotic situation. I also thought about Lharkin without whose motivation my attitude would have been a fighting one.

The monitoring screens showed satisfactory results. The impact of the micro-organisms was spreading, and the conditions were very suitable for their growth. The seeds were laid, and a new civilization was on the verge of its existence. Though it still required time, however our mission was on track. We had managed all the critical parts from execution to perfection and now we were to wait for the seeds to grow.

Chapter 7
Now We Wait

The needle of time is a magic stick. The more rounds it takes, the more magical it gets. Even if we have the figures and calculate the probabilities, visualizing sensations and undergoing experiences are time-defined states. We were witnessing spirituality from a completely different perspective, a perspective I'm yet to define.

The 5118208 was dry and lifeless. It had the water and living organisms, but life in terms of emotion and purpose was non-existent. The 5118208 was gradually terraforming. Everything in the eco-system seemed to have revived and enhanced. The evolutionary terraforming was the first of its kind. I was confident that the temperature stats and growth indices were in line with the ideal thresholds calculated through our research. The glory of science was overdone by the beauty of the experience.

5118208 was gradually shaping its environment in a way that was suitable for animals and plants to grow. The task of us as scouts was to visit the 5118208 on the defined schedules and monitor all the processes taking place there. Since I was in charge of the scout team accompanying me, I was the one who made their schedules. This allowed me to schedule the frequency of my trips. We had devices that were developed to compare the readings obtained through sensors. Those values indicated if the environment and climate for the micro-organisms were healthy enough to enable growth.

I hadn't stopped missing home. But I had come to terms with it. I tried to keep myself busy. And whenever I got on the 5118208, it felt amazing to be there. This place was silent and vacant, but to see it being filled gradually with the addition of colors to its life was amazing. Although the crash of the meteoroid had taken dinosaurs with it, it had also taken away the colors of nature and the concept of inhabiting the place. I would just think about how soon all of it was to change. The micro-organisms were serving its purpose and the process of growth had begun.

The Elders were pleased that the execution was perfect. I always had trust in them, just as they had in me. I knew if they had chosen this planet, they had done it for a reason. I was not specifically interested in what the reason was because I knew that whatever it was, it was never going to go against our gains. The Elders believing that I could do the job, made me realize that I could actually do it. I was becoming part of something great. I had something to look up to. Father would have been very proud. He should have been here to see how his research had led us to new prospects of life. He loved what he did. It's not that we did not have his affection or time, but I admired how he worked night and day to discover life and the universe.

After the climatic testing phase, it was time for sample testing. In the first phase, all we had to do was take along devices that had sensors built in them as only the climatic conditions were to be monitored. Once a cycle was to complete, it was to ensure the conditions would be ideal for the nourishment of newly born species. And so, it did. The sample testing was to verify if the micro-organisms had made the most of the weather, enabling the species to augment.

The samples we collected were to be tested in our lab at the spaceship. The lab specialists, who had not had many tasks assigned to them, prior to the testing phase, were to get busy in testing the samples. I posted two teams that had to visit the 5118208 on alternate weeks to get samples for the lab scientists. I was part of both the teams We would get ten random samples on every visit. Also, the deputation and scheduling of teams were based on locations. We had to ensure the entire planet had an environment that enabled the micro-organisms to function.

I was the only scout who had traveled the 5118208 prior to the terraforming. Most of them were fascinated to see the 5118208 change. I had been there, but then it was a different place and now it was in transition. The scouts accompanying me on the monitoring mission had similar stories as I had. Some were married, some in love, and a few experiencing space life, for the first time. There was one thing in common, and that was the passion to step beyond Trinity and explore space. Since we were there for an uncertain length of time, we had become more of a family, a space family. It was nice to be surrounded by people who were excited and who had made somewhat similar sacrifices as I had.

Finally, it was time to collect samples of plants and animals. It was a very exciting process and the entire scout team under my command was to visit the 5118208 and gather samples from different species. There was no limit besides time. The sample could be obtained from species growing in water or land. The range of species had multiplied to a great extent. Every time we returned, we found more species than we had found the previous time. The other scouts were also blown away with the versatility of flower patterns. They were mostly amused by the water species. The samples of water species were to be taken in containers with water. It had all become very adventurous.

The jobs of the scouts had increased. The sample collection and its analysis were all included in the tasks of the scouts. Also, as the range of species was extremely vast as predicted, the number of scouts did not seem sufficient for the task. I had told the Elders prior to leaving that more scouts would be needed when the time came, and the time had finally come.

I got in contact with the Elders and briefed them about the situation. They always showed trust in me and they realized that since everything had happened as per plan, it was indeed time to increase the number of scouts working on the spaceship. The spaceship we had did not have much room for more than fifteen scouts.

"Tuloriah, you can have as many scouts as you want," the Elder assured me.

"I would need fifty more. Also, the provisions won't last for long," I replied.

"You will have them soon," they answered, and the augmented call disconnected.

I did not know how many more trained scouts were available back in Trinity. Even if they weren't trained, I could train them, and the Elders were aware of it. They did not say it, but I am sure it was in their knowledge.

I ensured that the resources were utilized in the best of manner. A few of the scouts had even become homesick. They wanted to go back as all their excitement had died down. Out of the lot, I was the only one who was sent who would not return. The others weren't told how long they were to stay. As we waited eagerly for the spaceship to arrive, the 5118208 was phenomenally transforming. It had become extremely colorful and the animals had adapted to the climate extremely well. The destruction that was witnessed right after extinction of dinosaurs was replaced by lively colors, and refreshing sounds of nature. The random collection of samples was to be strategized in accordance with regions, and that could only be done when the spaceship arrived since the number of scouts was not sufficient.

We had stopped our visits, as a detailed structural plan was required to gather information and samples in a systematic order. The random collection could lead to confusion, which is why I paused the visits to the 5118208 waiting for more help to arrive.

It did not take the Elders long to formulate a team. The spaceship had finally arrived and this one was a lot larger than the one we were on. The spaceship closed in and stopped at a fair distance. We generated an impulse to enquire about the number of members and the return schedule of either of the spaceships. The impulse was received, and in a matter of time, a reply was signaled. The reply had the information that the ship had one hundred trained scouts. The ship we were on was to return. The members of my team were at free will and could return if they wanted to. I was to stay. Soon they generated another impulse that the spaceship captain wanted to speak to me in person. He dropped out and we helped him inside our spaceship.

"Pleasure to meet you, Ms Tuloriah. My name is Sarawak and I have been sent by the Elders to deliver the scouts to you and brief you on this matter. Before we start speaking about the scouts and the project, I just want you to know that you're my inspiration."

His comments had revived the sense of leadership and greatness my responsibility composed in itself. It was as if on the spaceship traveling to and from the 5118208, I had forgotten about how The Trinity was, I hadn't.

"Welcome Sarawak. That is very kind of you. It was because of the Elders I was able to make a difference, if I was able to make any at all. You may proceed with the message," I responded.

He told me that the ones to stay would have to move to the spaceship that had just arrived. It had more capacity and sufficient provisions for a very long period. The ones who wanted to pack and move the other spaceship were given a six-hour notice to pack up as then the first spaceship was to return. I thanked everybody for the respect and service. One of the lab specialists had told me he wanted to leave. I gave him a flower to deliver to my Lharkin. It was only he and one other scout who returned, the others said they wanted to stay with me. I was very pleased to see them respond with so much affection and respect. We packed our belongings and traveled in the spaceship we were in to the one that had arrived a few hours before.

The other spaceship was huge. It had over thirty rooms. Each room was to be shared by three scouts. I was also assigned an assistant since the number of people under my command had multiplied. I never had asked for one, but I definitely could use some more help.

As soon as I boarded the new ship, I called for an urgent briefing. There was a huge hall that could be addressed to from the top. That space was needed as a large number of scouts could never have gathered in any other place. They were all new faces, and since I was at a fair height to be visible to everybody present, it was even harder to distinguish the faces. I reminded them of the purpose we were there for. We were not there to fight or cause any further destruction, we were there to bring 5118208 to new life.

The enthusiasm and excitement of the newly arrived scouts could evidently be seen through their expressions. It gave me an idea about how the people of Trinity admired our courage of living away from our families for the sole purpose of laying the foundation of a new habitual civilization. It was overwhelming.

"What you will see is an experience you might never have imagined. The sights might never have existed in your minds as what you are to see is something your imagination might never have pictured."

I ended my speech on that note and walked back into my chamber. Also, in my speech, I had informed the scouts that new trips were to be scheduled in no time. I placed the experienced members of our teams as team leaders and created eight teams Five teams were designated to collect samples from the water that covered a huge part of the 5118208 mainly in five areas. The other three teams were assigned to visit the land regions. The regions included the central, northern, and southern region. The number of species was amazingly high. Additionally, the repetition of the samples was to occur.

While we were forming teams and designating

tasks, the animals and plants on 5118208 had matured to a great degree. The ones visiting it the first time were not the only ones that were to be surprised. It was time for the first visit, after the new teams' formation. We had set a timeline and that timeline was to be followed strictly in order to be certain that all corners of the planet had been studied.

When I landed on the planet after a long break, the sights were breathtaking. Even though our image processing system was able to replicate the vector images, it still did not portray the images as they were due to the ozone layer formed. When I got there, the colors and textures of various animals and plants were mesmerizing.

On every visit, we discovered something new. The discovery and monitoring phase was a side by side process. The micro-organisms had indeed proved to be the best. There was a reason why the Elders were so proud of me and I could easily see it after witnessing how it helped animals and plants grow. I only imagined how the 5118208 would look when millions and millions of species survived there. I wondered how life on 5118208 would be different from life on Trinity. Only time was to tell.

Every species was different from the ones we had at Trinity, whether an animal species or plant species. There was a slight similarity in some ways, but the colors and textures of the species of 5118208 were very sharp and fine. The other scouts were also amazed as they had never seen such animals and plants before. They had never thought of visualizing such colorful organisms that not only looked different from the ones we had at The Trinity, but also the range of the species was immaculate. There were animals that resembled each other, yet were extremely different in size, shape, and other characteristics. The water species were very unique. In Trinity, every species that existed in water could survive on land, but on 5118208, the case was different.

Most of the water species could not survive on land, and the few that could, were the only ones of that kind. It was enthralling to see the micro-organism grow animals and plants so differently. We hadn't stopped monitoring, and everything was going fine.

I told the Elders about how the project was progressing. Lharkin was right about everything. He was right that I was chosen because I had what was required to ensure that the process was a success. If I hadn't taken the responsibility, things could have been different. I might have not experienced how it felt to be on 5118208. I might have missed the beautiful living things and deep down in my heart, I was thankful to the Elders for choosing me. I knew that this is what I was born for.

Chapter 8
Fallen Angels

Every experience has a unique lesson to learn from. Not all experiences are difficult to comprehend. Neither is it possible to accelerate the learning process, things happen at their own time. The difference of experiences is based on the willingness to explore and expedite. Maybe I was never meant to restrict myself from stretching beyond self-defined limitations. I did not have control over the result of the process and success of the mission. Something could have randomly gone wrong, but it didn't. That's how life is, thrilling and unpredictable.

Out of all the phases, the monitoring phase was the most critical one. If the right conditions were not maintained, the possibility of the survival of the micro-organisms would have been out of the question. All the tasks prior to the initiation of the monitoring period were executed to perfection without any complications. We made sure nothing went wrong.

The monitoring phase was in its completion. We had noticed that the environment was self-sustainable and serving the micro-organism's growth effectively. Gradually species had come into existence and a bare land full of giant creatures was replaced by species of mostly miniature animals and plants when compared. The species were not designed and placed with any regard to their size, shape or adaptability. The environment was to provide them with minerals and nutrition, which were to design their texture and physical features. It was confirmed that living things could survive and thrive on planet 5118208.

The Elders were glad that all our calculations were right and timely executions had allowed the mission to be a success. It was only the beginning. Even though the place was suitable for living things, however it did not confirm that the environment could aid civilizations and masses of people living together. The Elders had to come up with a solution.

After the monitoring period, we were asked to return to The Trinity. I was called upon by the Elders to brief them about project 5118208 and indicate concerns, if there were any. I told the Elders that everything was perfectly fine and that our executions and evaluations collectively had ensured that we were heading in the right direction. However, I had my concerns regarding the existence and sustainability of human life. The Elders were aware of it and were interested to know if I had a solution in mind. I tried to ask and find out, but the only thing I was told was to advise solutions and not enquire about them.

I had not expected to return. Once the monitoring period was over, I was surprised when I was asked by the Elders to return. The mixed emotions of happiness and fear revisited me. It was very difficult for me to part with my family on the last meeting and it had consumed a lot of my energy to digest it. The return was everything I could have asked for, but the uneasiness of having to return was making me paranoid. The day we landed on The Trinity, I rushed to my family. Before confronting my Lharkin, I prepared myself to hold onto any emotions of love. As soon as I saw him, at the moment I felt nothing had changed and that we hadn't ever parted.

The only thing he asked was if I had to return. I nodded my head telling him I had to, he gave me a hug and did not argue.

The council sessions between the Elders were conducted on a regular basis to come up with a solution to test 5118208 for humans. Since I had no suggestions to offer, I did not attend any of those meetings. I was not trying to figure out solutions. I was happy with the delay in the process as I was getting to spend more time with my family. The longer the decision making was going to take, the longer I could be home, with Lharkin.

In a matter of a few days, I was told that I was to return and re-confirm that the conditions were perfect to start societies of human beings. The news had shaken me, similar to how it had done the first time I was leaving. The only difference was that on the last occasion I wasn't told that I would never return. There was a very slight chance of seeing my family again. This time, they had confirmed that I could never come back. Those were my final days on Trinity, and I was to travel away with all my memories.

The Elders had decided whom they were going to send for experimentation. I was glad it wasn't me. The chosen ones were scouts who weren't considered decent. The scouts were mainly people who had committed crimes or had a reputation for bad behavior. They were to be sent there and the only thing which awaited their departure was my confirmation.

The scouts being sent were not happy with the decision. They wanted to live in The Trinity. They were born and raised in The Trinity. They were satisfied with their living conditions and all the bounties they had on their planet. Most of them were terrified to go away and live in a place which wasn't ideally suitable for them. A few of them even resisted, but there was nothing they could have done as the Elders had made up their minds.

The day of our departure was around the corner. The way I expected a delay in the process was then the condition of the scouts who were to travel and live in the 5118208. My family had barely got accustomed to seeing me again, but there was nothing I could have done to change the situation. I was again in dire need of support and gladly Lharkin was there to provide me with it.

He could sense I wasn't comfortable about leaving my family. Somewhere my heart wanted to continue the mission and the period I had spent while we were distant had pulled me out of denial.

"What are you going to do here? The stars and galaxies are the place for you," he would tell me. His words weren't just comforting statements, but it was his meaningful and sincere advice. I could tell it by looking into his eyes.

When the Elders asked me if I needed a few more days, I said no. Why would I make it all harder for myself? The sooner I was to leave, the easier it was going to be. The scouts wouldn't have liked my decision if they had any idea that I was willing to get back to my spaceship and send in a confirmation report. The 5118208 was nothing like The Trinity. The planet was full of water which was a result of the reaction and besides that, greenery and ice covered most of the land. In Trinity, waterfalls were accompanied by wine falls and juice falls. The fruits in Trinity were delicious and had over twenty million species; not one of them was present on 5118208.

On the way back, I decided to pretend nothing was wrong, but as days passed, my control on my emotions was fading away. Nature has a give-and-take law. It never gives you anything without taking something away from you. It is a direct proportionality between what you desire and what you have to give in order to have your desire fulfilled. Despite having a different reputation, my situation was quite similar to the situation of the scouts. Maybe mine was worse. I was leaving The Trinity forever just as they were, but they were going to live in a new environment while I was to spend the rest of my life in a spaceship. It is said one can never be satisfied with what they get, well I couldn't agree more.

There was a brighter side to my job. I was the scout who was to lead the project and make critical decisions. The Elders were proud of my performance and commitment. There was a great responsibility on me, and it was something I always wanted. Since my childhood, I was interested in the stars and always wanted to be out there in the galaxies. As a child, I even prayed to spend my entire life there. My father would laugh whenever I said that, and neither of us would have ever known that my prayer was answered then and there, and I was to live on a spaceship for the rest of my life.

While growing up my love for space only increased, but the idea of being there forever without ever returning was never part of my ambitions or plans. I never imagined life to be this way. The Elders knew that the decision was not going to be easy for me which is why they asked me if I needed more time. My trust in the Elders had never perished. I knew if they had chosen me to take charge of the project, they knew I was capable.

I was born in The Trinity and I loved everything about the planet. Although the galaxies attracted me, however whenever I set off for an expedition, deep down I knew I was soon to return. It was something I had inherited from my father. I grew up listening to his stories of how the galaxy was. Subconsciously I always knew my home was not on the ground of any planet, even Trinity for that matter. If I were to choose a planet to live, I would have definitely opted for the planet I was born and raised in. Not only because of my family and acquaintances, but also the weather and the environment.

The scouts chosen were not picked from a particular region of The Trinity but were people coming from all across the three planets. They were disappointed that they had to start all over again and adjust to the conditions of the 5118208. They were already people who were not liked by the society. It didn't matter why they were not liked, they were most probably people who were not willing to adapt or compromise and sending them away was what they deserved.

I decided to speak to Lharkin about moving on as he was to spend life in my absence. I knew he would never agree and would prefer spending the rest of his life living memories which had both of us in them. It was going to be a difficult conversation, but in order to attain closure, I had to get through with it.

It was my last day on The Trinity and I told him that there was something I wanted to speak to him about. He might have guessed a lot of things, but asking him to marry another woman was surely out of the question.

We sat on the stone chair which was right outside our door. We often sat there and discussed life while gazing at the stars. It was not dark. The brightness of the day was contradicting my dark emotions.

I held his hand and said, "We are never going to be with each other again. This is our last meeting."

He gave me a tender smile and replied, "I might not be with you, but you will stay in my heart forever. I want you to know this, I'm really happy for you. It will be difficult, but you will do great, I'm sure."

His words had made me too weak to put forward my argument. I looked him in the eyes with tears streaming down my cheeks. "I love you and I want you to make a promise."

He laughed and said, "Anything you say."

I told him I wanted him to get married. He did not like the idea and disagreed. He said that there wasn't a need for it. The conversation was very difficult and was not leading to any results. I was forcing him but was unable to penetrate through his resistance. It was maybe a bit too much I was asking for. He knew best what he wanted, and he definitely needed more time to think it over. Rushing him to conclusions was not going to help him in any way. The moment I realized it, I changed my demand. I asked him to promise me that he would at least think about marrying after I left. It was the least I could do.

I was prepared to leave. Lharkin insisted on traveling to the space station with me, but I asked him to stay behind. I did not want to become weak in the last moments of my departure. People living in The Trinity were surrounded by millions of people. There were families which existed there. Even if I was somebody who lived alone and did not have a family, to live thousands of miles away with a slew of strangers was going to be challenging. In my case, I was somebody who was surrounded by people and was always engaged in the community. I was asked to see the Elders before my last take-off from The Trinity.

When I entered the meeting room where most of the council meetings were conducted, the members of the cabinet stood up showing the respect they had for me. Then they stated that they were very proud of me and that the entire planet was in debt to me for my services. I felt honored.

I thanked them for their support and kind words. I gave them a precise briefing about the timeline and plan of action. They discussed with me how they were waiting for my signal to send in the scouts they had gathered from all regions of The Trinity, which were to be taken to the 5118208. I was to visit the 5118208 with them. It was my last physical meeting with the Elders. They were to stay in contact with me, but it was our last corporeal confrontation.

I walked towards the spaceship and boarded it. I was accompanied by fifteen members, eight of whom were to return after the placement of the scouts. The other seven were deployed for an uncertain length of time. I was commissioned to monitor the 5118208 till eternity.

I left there and sent in a confirmation within a few days' time. I had to ensure that the conditions were not deadly, and they weren't. I also had to finalize the locations where they were to be placed. After closely monitoring, I chose the central region as the conditions there were most balanced. The scouts were sent there and were asked to start a new life. The eight team members had returned, and there were eight of us left on the spaceship.

We were to monitor the scouts as it was too early to gauge whether or not it was safe for the existence of the human race. It was a lot of hard work and research that had got us this far. We could only hope for these scouts not to turn into dinosaurs, leading us back to where we started.

It was a new beginning for all of us who had left The Trinity. It was not something any of the scouts would have considered ideal. The best thing to do then was to conform to reality and make the best out of it rather than mourning over leaving The Trinity. I was determined to move on and focus as it was the best way to progress. My team members' mindset was similar to mine as I regularly counseled them to be dedicated. There was nothing they could have done to change their reality. They were destined to be part of something great and this itself was enough for them to move on.

Chapter 9
Hybrid

As days were passing by, we focused on monitoring the conditions and witnessed the evolution of the species. Evolution is a long-term process and things never evolve overnight. According to our research, the species were to take a thousand years to reach a state we had conceptualized. The transitional phases were only going to lead to our conceptualization if they happened conformingly and we were there to ensure that it happened that way.

The scouts we had sent down were doing fine and were settling down to extreme conditions. The temperature of the 5118208 was maintained for the micro-organisms to grow. For the detainee scouts who were sent on the 5118208, the weather condition was not very suitable. They moved to the poles of the 5118208. It was the place where the Neanderthals explored at the very end. Until it was to be explored, they were to wait for them.

The next few weeks were slow. We could see the species of the Neanderthals growing, but they hadn't completely gotten into shape. It was amazing to see them transform. The Neanderthals looked like apes.

They were created using the DNA of apes with room for improvement or rather evolution. They looked different and behaved differently.

Soon the 5118208 was crowded with Neanderthals. They were hairy. Their legs were short when compared to their bodies. Their physique was very stocky. They were broad and thick with erect, big noses. They all looked quite similar and it was difficult to distinguish between them.

They needed time to understand their environment. When a large number of Neanderthals came into existence, the 5118208 had become a wild place. For them it was strange, they had to struggle for survival and did not know how they were to live. They had to figure out everything. What they were to eat, where they were to get it from, and even how they were to eat it.

I learned hunger is a self-training skill. It was a trait, humans were born with. It was what taught the Neanderthals survival. The first of these Neanderthals wildly ran around, hoping that running would kill their need of hunger or even satiate it, for that matter. They were unable to decode the feeling of hunger as something that needed nutrition and food to be suppressed. When they realized that they had to consume something physically, they looked around and tried eating anything they got their hands on. Be it stones or sand, they tried having it all.

Failing over being able to have anything, they targeted the species of plants. Plants were soft, had a taste, and were easier to chew and swallow down. Not every plant had a decent taste and was nutritious enough. They tried different species until they found themselves the one which was good in taste and killed their hunger. There was no uniformity in their choice. Every Neanderthal chose its own plant species. Initially, there was no understanding between them mainly because they lacked communication.

They did not have any sense of their location and they tried staying close to their food as they did not want to remain hungry. That's what humans are, and food is all they work for, whether it was forty thousand years ago or the human beings who currently live on this planet. It all begins with food and ends just about at it.

With time, their population increased, and they discovered that they could consume animals as well. They were exploring everything around them. The animal species they tried having were tastier and way more nutritious than the plants. They did not know much about the nutritious aspect, and all they felt was a filled stomach. It was not something that happened in a standardized manner. Not all the Neanderthals were learning about different types of food together. It was a haphazard process, but eventually, all of them did.

Food was not the only thing they had to learn about. Since we had planted these micro-organisms all across the 5118208, so was their existence. The amazing difference between them lay in their bodies. The ones who lived in hot regions had less hair and had thinner flesh, while the ones who lived in the colder regions had a lot of hair and had thick skin. Even then, survival was not a very easy task, they had to learn to protect themselves from the scorching sun and the ones living in cold regions had to battle out the cold winds.

They had completed the first phase successfully. It was their survival. The Neanderthals living in different parts of the 5118208 had learned to eat, find their food and counter extreme weather conditions when required. It was still a long way to go, but the long way was subject to their survival.

We, the scouts, were closely watching them from our spaceship. It was amazing to see them learn and make their way for a living. They naturally had the urge to breed, which is why their population constantly kept on increasing. As the population increased, so did the discoveries since more Neanderthals meant more minds. Nothing was changing in terms of their physique. They still had short legs and huge bodies, but then, it was not our main concern.

Even the hairiest of them were very different from apes. They were not completely covered with hair, as was the case with apes. It was funny how they were smart, yet not smart enough to be aware of their smartness. The example of their sharp minds was how they hid under trees to protect themselves from rain and the boiling sun. Also, they were gradually learning to differentiate between edible and non-edible food. They had stopped searching for food in everything and had formulated their own criteria for the selection of food. For instance, they crushed food to see if it was or was not digestible.

A few years passed and nothing much changed in their behavior. It was about time for us to make the move. We had trained celestial scouts to bond with these Neanderthals once they got into better shape. After a few years, their physique had improved, and they had become a fraction more civilized. It seemed as though they had reached their limit of exploration and needed further assistance to grow. The assistance could only be given if the future generations inherited genes which were unique. In order to insert such genes in their blood, the celestial scouts were sent off from Trinity to the 5118208.

The scouts sent were over eleven hundred in number. The scouts chosen were all injected with bacteria which created heat in their body. This was done to make them attracted to the Neanderthals as well as allowing their bodies to stay healthy in comparatively different weather conditions. The excess of hydrocarbons, which had caused to change the climatic conditions of the 5118208 was not very suitable for us scouts. This had been verified in the monitoring period of the people sent. However, it was not a life threat.

The focus of the Elders lied in making 5118208 a community of new human species. In order to attain that, the hypersexuality of the scouts being sent had to be enhanced. After injecting the bodies of the trained scouts, they were directly sent to the 5118208 from Trinity. The scouts were no different from the people sent earlier as they were all members of the society who did not conform to its norms. They were the ones who were not considered to be decent. The only difference was that they were labeled as scouts since they had volunteered to be part of the process, unlike the ones sent earlier.

The bacteria did not only impact their internal capabilities but also changed their physical structure to a certain degree. Their skin color had been toned down. The purpose of doing so was to ensure the Neanderthals did not attack them, but rather became attracted to them. The injection was to react after a few hours of its use. The scouts were provided with a special seat in the spaceship, which was to take them there. The special seats were all covered in glass and had nothing but an appropriate ratio of gases inside it. The ratio of the gases was in contrast to the gases present on 5118208.

They were dropped on to the 5118208 on locations where the Neanderthals existed. Even though they existed almost in every part of the 5118208 beside the poles, it was not very difficult to release them in a scattered manner. Most of the 5118208 was covered with water as a result of the reaction. The micro-organisms were synthesized in a way that they could only live on land, which meant that the scouts were only to be dropped on one-third of the 5118208.

The scouts landed in different regions and

approached the Neanderthals. As per the Elders' evaluation, the Neanderthals were attracted to these Trinity humans which were then transformed. The mating process between the two different species began. Over a short time, a new species of humans was conceived. All the scouts sent were male, so only the Neanderthals could conceive. Days passed by and the Neanderthals produced babies. The babies were slightly different. It was all part of the evolution. For them to be as different as the humans today, it took a period of thousands of years, if not less.

The new babies grew into having longer legs than their fathers, but the difference among the firstborn was minimal. Their bodies were huge which required time to get into a balanced shape. The newly born cross-bred babies were a lot saner than their ancestors. They grew up to be smarter and found different kinds of foods. It was the first time that fruits were discovered by the human species on this planet. With the passage of time, the babies grew into fully grown humans, yet not in the best structure. They mated and the new generations born through their mating were better looking.

Subsequently, hundreds of years passed by and the Neanderthal humans learned the process of planting seeds. They figured how the seeds were buried in soil and grew on their own. Then, rain carried out irrigation and the sun provided them with all the nutrients necessary. The 5118208 was becoming a better place to live. They mainly grew and consumed barley. There were other crops and fruits as well on the list of items they had learned to plant and cultivate.

Their living conditions had also changed. They had centered in limestone caves. The caves were sort of societies a hundred thousand years ago. They had become cavemen. There were multiple reasons why they preferred staying in the caves; one of them was the fact that the cave was immune to extremes of hot and cold temperatures. Also, living in the open air would make them subject to hungry predators which were limited animal species. After another hundred years, their structure changed to a great degree. Their legs and bodies grew to be almost of the same size. Also, the features of their face differentiated from the features of the apes, or the first Neanderthals for that matter.

The reason the early Neanderthals resembled the apes was because the DNA of the micro-organisms was formed using the DNA of the apes. The crossbreeding with the people of The Trinity had altered the physical aspects of the DNA and had enhanced the cognitive functionality of the then born species. The later generations had facial features which were completely different from their ancestors, the earliest Neanderthals.

I was watching everything happening on the spaceship. It was phenomenal to see them evolve. I had witnessed different phases of their transformation and what excited me was the fact that their evolution process was not complete. It was a thousand years ago, at least, when I was very eager to see how they would end up looking.

It was interesting to see them learn to dress. They had slowly but surely become aware of how important it was for them to hide their genitals. They first used big leaves to cover their bodies. They mainly covered their genitals and nothing else. Once they learned to cover their bodies, they realized that they could use other substances to cover their bodies, such as animal skin. This helped them stay dry in rain and covered in extreme cold. The caves were already protecting them from the difficulties caused by rain and extreme temperatures, but it was about moving a step further.

With time, they moved out of caves and started creating their own homes. The homes then were only made with big tree branches. Home meant having shade and nothing more. When they learned to live in the open by creating their houses, they soon started expanding their habitats. The boundaries of living around areas where there were caves were eliminated. These human species started living along seashores and in open deserts. Their lifestyle was very nomadic as they did not spend much time in one place. This was how they travelled to the extreme corners of the planet and even ended up confronting the people living in those regions. They mated with them and gradually their generations evolved quite similarly to the rest.

I remember how the invention of the wheel completely changed their lives. By then they had started living in a more civilized manner. At that time, they learned to settle down and live together as a community. There were no such socially defined norms or civilized behavioral characteristics like humans have today. They had just begun to live in concentrations according to where food and water were readily available. Each man and woman provided for themselves and their children as it had been since their existence.

The wheel, however, had worked as a catalyst in their evolutionary process. It was at that time they explored different aspects of communication. Prior to verbal communication, the human species communicated in sign language. They had signs for everything. With time the sign language was further modernized to a written sign language. Through symbols, they carried out detailed discussions and the sign language was restricted for basic communication. At the time of the invention of the wheel, they had started communicating in voice, but that voice communication was based on sounds. The humankind living in different regions of the planet had standardized their communicational parameters differently. This was what made them resist continuously travelling as whenever they ended up in a new place, they had to learn new signs, and sounds later on.

According to the human calculation, which is somewhat close but not precise, it was in the early 2000s when they mastered the art of communication. This was when they had become fluent in speaking and had developed a hierarchal structure. It was then that they fought over resources and tried to expand their territory and things for humans have been that way ever since.

It was at this time that they had transformed into better looking, smart human beings. Their legs were long and their bodies masculine, yet not huge. They were not covered in hair as they used to be, and their faces had completely evolved. They did not have big noses and their lips had become delicate and attractive.

It was amazing to see the evolution, from laying micro-organisms on the planet to witness them evolve into smart human beings. It took a lot of time as was expected, but the results were indeed very satisfactory. From having a lifespan of over a hundred years, with time, their lifespans kept on decreasing. The elders had predicted that they were creating a human species, which would ultimately have a short lifespan and would evolve to civilized humans. They had begun writing things down and gaining knowledge. They had started experimenting with nature and its provisions, and just like their visible features, their mind had also become sharp and intelligent.

The communities, or rather societies, formed in the later aeons were way more disciplined. It was no longer a group of naked wild people living together; instead, it was a society of people living together in a respectable way. The evolution was not over, but the pace of it had definitely increased. Most of the humans of that era did not even know what their ancestors, the Neanderthals, looked like.

Chapter 10
Gods

The people had evolved to a great degree. It was time for another visit. The Elders had formed a team of scouts who were to visit 5118208 to see and report on the progress. Progress could evidently be seen as I had a close eye on it. I also kept the Elders updated as to how it was changing, but the time had come to visit the 5118208 and see what more was required to improve the living conditions of the humans at that time.

The scouts landed on the island of Atlantis. The human species had also been living there. The picture of the landing of the celestial scouts was amazing. Every human who witnessed it was astounded by the visuals. Humans were not accustomed to technology at that time. For them, the technology was unfathomable. They were amazed to see the spaceship land on the shore of the island. The spaceship made a huge noise and the sound at first had drawn their attention. When the huge spaceship landed, every human living on the island was present there.

Soon, the scouts walked out, and the people of the area were even more surprised. The scouts getting off the spaceship were completely different from the human race. There was no resemblance between them; little could they know that their genes were inherited from people who were from where the celestial scouts belonged. The scouts were well-equipped and had communication devices with them. They were amazed at how the scouts contacted each other through those devices and worked on virtual screens. For the people of Trinity, it was nothing extraordinary, but the case on 5118208 was not the same.

The visit to Atlantis was sufficient for the scouts as through that location, they could easily study how the other humans were doing. The need for travelling to different locations was not necessary as they had brought along all devices which were needed to collect data from other places.

After the first visit, the scouts thought that humans lacked the technology, and that the addition of technology could transform their lives. They had reached a point from which advancements were not possible in the absence of technology. On the other hand, it was to be understood that if the humans suddenly got their hands on technology, they were most likely to misuse it. It would transition the evolution into a revolution. Evolution is a slow step-by-step process while revolution is something that happens abruptly. For humans, evolution has been the key as revolutions have led them to destruction instead of casting a positive impact.

The first visit lasted for seven 5118208 months.

The scouts then returned. The people living on Atlantis, on seeing the scouts, had fled away to a fair distance. It was the first time that people developed the concept of gods. For people who had witnessed them, the scouts were gods. A few groups of people disagreed and considered them as some unique species. The visits continued and so did the reporting process. The evolution of the 5118208 was very successful and interesting. Every time the scouts visited the 5118208, they felt the 5118208 and people living in it had matured, evolved and improved. What still stood their way of advancing a step further was the absence of technology, which the scouts were not sure to how they were going to fulfill.

The scouts had paid several visits until one of the scouts planned to stay in the city of Atlantis and not return. The scout believed that the 5118208 would definitely become a better place with technology and he decided to bring that technology to 5118208. The scout settled on the island of Atlantis and planned on making it the technological hub.

The scout had brought up all the equipment and developed the city of Atlantis in accordance with technology. People, fearing the scout to be a god, had left the island, and the next important thing was to get people there. The island was nothing like any other part of the world. What the scout had not realized was that the technology was too much for the people of the 5118208 to handle.

The scout did not have the permission of the Elders and he did not bother seeking it. Since he had not discussed it with the Elders, he had not weighed all the consequences. He did not even have a proper plan. The only thing the city had was technology and the scout lived there alone. After installing all the technological equipment, as much as he had and could, he focused on attracting people. It was not going to be an easy task as the people were fearful. By the time the scout could get things running, the Elders had received the news that the scout had not left. I had also informed the Elders that one of the scouts had stayed there. The Elders wanted to see what the scout was up to and once they realized what his plans were, the Elders decided to counter his approach.

The Elders knew that if the humans got their hands on the technology it was going to lead to terrible consequences. The humans did not need a revolution of any sort. It had taken humans hundreds and thousands of years to evolve; it could all be destroyed in a matter of seconds only because of the misuse of the resources by one scout. The Elders could not let that happen and they decided to take charge of things themselves instead of sending a team of scouts. The scout had already rebelled by not conforming to the Elders' orders and they did not want the problem to expand or escalate, which is why they decided to take care of things by themselves.

By the time the Elders departed, the scout had

already attracted humans and a civilization had begun on the island of Atlantis. The people took the scout as their supreme leader. They believed in what they saw, and since they had seen the scout bring technology, for them he was their god. The equipment and techniques the humans witnessed were beyond their imagination and they had every reason to believe the scout to be a supreme power. The men enjoyed playing around with technology and had no idea regarding its potential. Technology was a game for them. They did not know its purpose, nor did they care to enquire.

The scout had trained men and equipped them with technology. The men were labelled as Titans. The Titans were groomed and given the right amount of attention. They were trained so well by the rebellious scout that they had become a serious threat to the Elders. The radiations of technology were not at all suitable for the natural evolutionary process. Humans were eventually to become accustomed to technology but hastening the process could risk the entire project. Little did the scout care about the human civilization as he was swept away with the position that he had acquired for himself, the position of being god.

The Titans were armoured and were being mentally prepared for the war. The then Neanderthals, now humans, had a better understanding of emotions, something the earlier generations did not have. The scout gave motivational speeches and convinced his army that they were stepping into something great. It's not that the scout was being told from The Trinity about the attack that was going to be made on them, but he knew the Elders wouldn't let him get away with him going against their orders. The scout had no clue that he was playing a very dangerous game. For him, it was being the ruler of the people, a position he was never going to get in Trinity. Humans are born with a purpose, so were the scouts. The characteristics may differ, but their purpose was similar, which lies in following, instead of leading. A scout can lead a scout, and a human can lead a human. The problem arises when a cross connection is established. Humans are not and never were capable of leading the scouts, whereas the scouts could lead the humans (like the one who did). However, this was never going to last for a long time because the Elders — rightly so — would have never allowed things to proceed that way.

The scout was called "Amos". The number of men he had was gradually increasing and his army was gaining strength. He had further divided his army into groups and selected a few individuals who were to be trained as sub-leaders. He named one of them as Poseidon, one as Kleito and a few others. He trained them in such a way that it was not hard for the rest of the humans in his forces to believe that the ones the scouts had chosen were far more superior than the rest of the Titans. The scout became their main god, while the other chosen ones were the smaller ones. He was prepared for war and was expecting to be attacked by well-skilled scouts.

The Elders knew that the situation had become very difficult to tackle. They could have easily catalyzed a reaction that would have swept away half the population of the 5118208, specifically the people living in Atlantis. However, in this manner, the entire human race would have been at stake. The process that had transpired over hundreds and thousands of years would have all been in vain. I was prepared for war. I had dedicated my entire life to the project, and therefore I couldn't have allowed one scout to nullify all my sacrifices. All I needed were the orders of the Elders. I knew that if the Elders were to send any scout to regain the position of the technology and finish the technological civilization, it would be me.

The Elders had different plans; they knew that sending in scouts was too much of a risk. A technological war was to be disastrous itself, as the humans across the globe would have been at risk. They had to use the right amount of technology ensuring that both the problems were solved. When the Elders first told me that they were going to war by themselves, I felt a little disappointed because I really wanted to take down the scout myself. It was not going to be easy, but he had spoiled all my hard work, and if some scout were to take revenge it should have been me. Since I was a scout, I wasn't angered by their decision, yet I hoped to take part in it, in some way.

The Elders formulated a war strategy, better than

anyone ever could have done. The scout would have never thought he was to face the Elders and not a force of scouts. Had he known, he might have surrendered, if it were possible as he had got himself into a position from where turning back, was next to impossible. Had he done so, the first ones to bring him down would have been the leaders of Titans appointed by the scout himself. He had trained them way more than he should have. By the time he realized that he had trained them a bit too much, things had slipped out of hand.

The time had come for the first war on this planet. Prior to it, the 5118208 had never witnessed bloodshed. It was time for it to begin. The scout had appointed one of the Titans as their main leader who was also named the King of Atlantis by the scout, Amos. The others accepted him as their king only because Amos asked them to.

Humans until then were unaware of the concept of leadership and merit. It was the first time the human civilization was struck by hierarchies. They had freshly learned the basic family order which included wife and children, but that was all they were aware of. Amos educated them with traits of leaders and his distribution of the army opened up space for new social understandings.

The Elders attacked the city in no time and destroyed every bit of technology by simply sinking the city. Atlantis was surrounded by water and therefore, the Elders had planned to sink the island. It was an effective plan. The war was heralded as the war between gods and men. The Elders executed the plan to perfection. The city sank in no time and all the technological equipment went down with it. All the Titans drowned, and the Elders won the war. Even Amos was unable to save himself and died with the rest. The only people who survived were the chosen ones, for example, Poseidon and Cleito, who had gotten married and had ten sons. When they realized that they could never survive if they stayed there, they escaped the island before it sank. Cronos saw them escaping and followed them without risking his own life.

The Elders were aware of the ones who were escaping but they did not chase them down, which they easily could have done. Their main concern was to teach Amos a lesson for disobeying them and put an end to the technology that was harming the humans' evolutionary process. Once they were successful in doing so, they returned without causing any further damage.

After Atlantis fell, Cronos went to the Pharaohs directly. He told them about the city of Atlantis and asked for their help and support to rebuild a technologically advanced city. Before the war began, Cronos had suspected that they were going to be attacked by a powerful force. He sent his daughter and her husband Misor to a distant land towards the north so that they would be safe. Misor was the only priest in Atlantis and once he escaped, he found them and travelled with them to Egypt to meet the Pharaohs.

The Atlantean priest and Pharaoh Osiris worked together to create Egypt. After Misor died, his son Thoth and Osiris continued to build the incredible country. Thoth, the God of Egypt's history, kept all the stories about Atlantis that his father told. On one occasion, he told Osiris about the men and the scout who had destroyed their city. The story was passed on from one generation to another and even to this day, humans know about the first war on the planet. Naturally, they do not know the details as precisely as it happened as, over the years, the word has passed and been somewhat changed in the process. None of the humans know how the Elders, after killing the Titans who attacked them, positioned themselves on the corners of the island and pushed down so hard to the ground that the planet began to sink. I was on my spaceship witnessing it all.

"Men are mortal gods and gods are immortal men. Happy the man who understand these words, for he holds the key to all things." — The mystery of Osiris as expressed by him.

Chapter 11
Watchful Eyes

For centuries, I have been living in my spaceship watching over 5118208. I have witnessed various transitions within human civilization. The case with animals is not completely different. Even though quite a few animal species have gone extinct, there are others that have transformed and are very different from what they used to be a thousand years ago. Not only do they look different, they even behave differently.

The 5118208 has changed a great deal. I have witnessed the senseless Neanderthals, unaware and unresponsive to everything around them. I have witnessed humans of the 21st century, who are not only observant to technology, but are rather dependent on it. However, fundamentals haven't really changed to a great degree. The interpretation may be more accurate, yet the foundations remain the same. Every human, needs food, water, and shelter. The Neanderthals used living branches of trees, while humans use the dead branches. There is nothing that had altered in their biological selves. Physically though, their brains have grown incredibly. I must admit that even though I had expected extraordinary results, what I see now is way beyond my expectations.

With constant yet drastic changes on this planet, nothing much has changed in my duty and responsibilities. I have been monitoring and reporting the advancements of this planet. This spaceship has been my home. The things lying here that cannot speak or feel anything have heard all my cries and accompanied me in times when there was no one by my side. Various scouts have come and gone, but I have been in my spaceship, my home, for a very, very long time.

Sometimes I talk to myself for hours, and sometimes I even argue with myself. Since the last two hundred years, I have been alone, completely on my own. I could have asked for company and the Elders would have approved my request, but I never wanted someone here. Why would somebody else leave their family and live with me, in a place where solitude was not a choice but an option? Where loneliness had to be embraced and not challenged? I sacrificed a lot of things, and I do not regret doing so. It was my duty and responsibility to step up and be in charge and so I did.

Different spaceships have been sent from Trinity over different periods. The purpose of sending these spaceships is to remain aware of the rate of evolution. Evolution is a consistent process, and it has never stopped. It never will. Societies of humans will keep on improving and their learning capacity will only enhance. This is how the micro-organisms were designed to grow. The genes of exploration and desire to learn and the greed that drives them to want and have more will always be an essential part of human psychology.

The smartness of humans is worth appreciating. They have worked their way around technology quite nicely. They have become so capable that they even identify our visits. They refer to our spaceships as UFOs. The purpose of our visits is to be updated with the trends of this planet and always have control if things slip out of their hands. We are here to help them and not harm them. Humans don't really know that we are not a threat to them, but we haven't reached the point where we have to confront them and clarify that. Things are steady the way they are. Humans are yet not aware that our children study in their schools and work in their offices. They cannot know unless we want them to. They have been smart enough to pick up hints and do research on us, but to gain evidence, they are certainly miles away.

The Kepler 1625b is our spaceship designated to take kids from The Trinity to the universe. They are mainly sent to 5118208 for their research projects; however, the children aren't the only ones who are sent. As the data keeps on growing through research, I have realized that humans are just another version of the people living in Trinity. Although they appear different and have different beliefs, in the end, we are all humans. They are just a different species who have bodies different than ours. The rest is pretty much the same.

They have similar emotional connections with their families like we do. They are comfortable when they are surrounded by the same kind of people as they are, and there are a lot more similarities between them and us. Those similarities create a sense of acceptance. That's how we have accepted them, and they would too, the moment they learn that we are all the same.

Humans have the urge to learn and that urge has helped them to rationalize with the truth of the 5118208, providing them with logical justifications. Since they are yet to understand how they came into being, different theories circulate among different societies.

The word had passed from Thoth to the next generations one after another and will continue to pass on. Even though the generations today do not know what happened, but through research they have formulated theories, which are close to what really happened. The case with the majority is very different. Most of the humans assume that it was all the result of an explosion, and they explain it through the 'big bang theory'. I would completely call that wrong, as that explosion was a result of the chemical reaction I myself had initiated. Then there is a huge percentage who believe in different gods, most of which are nothing but self-created. Then again, I would not completely disagree either, as for them the Elders are gods, and well, since they created them, I can only agree.

What I have been amused by is the belief system.

Our belief system is the exact same as the humans'. Keeping religious and mythological beliefs aside, humans have our instincts and believe in rationalizing all aspects of the apparent reality. It would be wrong to compare the people living on the 5118208 with the people living on The Trinity since the 5118208 people have some of our genes but not all of them. They are unique in their own way, but their strengths are different. Their lifespans are short, and their social life is different. They are not at peace as we are. This was the only instinct they hadn't inherited. A thousand years ago, humans were not political, and they did not have the hunger for power. Today, the 5118208 is a dangerous place and the threat to human is nothing else, but humans.

I really hope we do not end up wiping out a sect of humans who are dedicated to creating unrest and creating a monopoly that suits them best, as is similar to what occurred during the first war on this planet, between Amos, his Titans, and the Elders. I am afraid with how things are proceeding, we might end up taking arms against them. We wouldn't do so to protect ourselves as we are far more equipped and capable than humans can ever be. We have created them, and we can always reverse our approach, but we would only do so to make this world a better place. I can sense that the time isn't far away when this happens, but I hope all my predictions prove wrong and the humans regard each other in a more humane manner.

Even today, when I look at this planet, it reminds me of the time when I first visited here. I used to be nervous and would wonder if all of this would ever pay off. I would even at times question my father's theories, doubting his research. As the process progressed, my doubts faded away and now I am only proud of my father. I'm sure he would have been proud of me the same way if he had seen his daughter connect the dots in the right manner. I guess he knew I would which is why he always kept me close to his work. Although he never said it, I know for sure that he knew I was just like him, curious, adventurous, and determined.

Finally, I have received a message from the Elders that I can revisit The Trinity and be reunited with my family. There are only a few more days until I depart. I have mixed co-existent emotions of love, excitement, and nausea. I wonder how much my son will have grown and how my husband will react after seeing me. I truly love my husband and his love is the purest affection I have ever received, but when you see somebody after a thousand years or so, you can only wonder how the meeting will go. I believe when you see somebody after such a long time, it feels as though you are meeting them for the first time. I believe this is another attribute we share with the humans, at least so far as what my research and analysis say.

The one I'm most excited to see is my son. I had left him and travelled at an age when he was a very young child. He wouldn't have got over my departure in such a short period as he was in a growing age. I wonder if my husband would have told him the truth or would he have lied to him and said that his mother had died. There are just endless possibilities of what all could have happened during the period I wasn't present in The Trinity. I never contacted him over the years, I could have but I did not because I did not want to make it more difficult for both him and me. I never knew I would ever get an opportunity to return and reunite with my family. If I knew, I would have definitely maintained contact.

After I left, the humans would never know that there was somebody there, watching over them from a thousand miles above. They would never know that they were being researched for thousands and thousands of years. They wouldn't have even known about my sufferings. Yes, I have been on a safe spaceship and have had everything I needed to survive but I have been alone throughout these years. It was my decision, and I wasn't forced to make it, but there were consequences. It's not that the Elders kept me in the dark or that I did not know that there would be hard times. I was expecting it, but I had to follow the orders of the Elders and, in the bigger picture, I had to fulfill the purpose of my existence. I was born to do so and so I did.

The glimpses of my last meeting with my family have always stayed with me. They were the only memories I have counted on and have been the fuel that has helped me move on. It was a very painful goodbye and I had left my house with tears in my eyes. Even after these thousand years, tears have never left me. Parents are all the same. Whether it be of any human species, whether living on the 5118208 or The Trinity, even when it comes to the species of animals, motherhood is the same for everyone. I remember how my son was sleeping in his cradle. I remember how he half-blinked his eyes in his sleep when I kissed his forehead. I remember how my husband resisted crying only because he did not want it to make any more difficult for me. I remember everything as if it had just happened yesterday.

In the last few days on this spaceship, all I can think of is how surprised my husband will be to see me return. I even fear of being surprised myself, but I know I will accept whatever might have happened. I knew whatever my husband did would have been for the right reason. I wanted him to unite with another woman and move on in life. He had promised me he wouldn't and all these years I had hoped that he broke his promise. Suddenly, after being informed that I was returning by the Elders, everything changed. I was used to living this way. It's not that I do not want to see my family again but digesting the news hasn't been easy either.

Nevertheless, I'm the only one who has witnessed all the phases of this planet. Different scouts came and went, the Elders visited once and have always been receiving reports from me, but none of them has constantly centered their concentration on the growth of this planet. If I claim that I know humans better than even the humans themselves, I can do so, as I have thousands of years to my credit.

The time has arrived where this long journey comes to an end. I might have to revisit the 5118208 or might set off on another expedition in a parallel universe. I might end up living with my family and spend the rest of my life with them. That is for time and the Elders to decide. I would always give my best as my father has taught me.

I sincerely hope that the people of this planet start being kind to themselves before things get way out of control and a foreign intervention becomes the only solution. It might put an end to the human civilization and even the process might have to be carried out all over again. Even if I don't live for that long, the Elders will train someone else, someone whom they believe has the potential. But before that happens, I hope people learn from their mistakes and make the 5118208 a better place to live.